GATHERING OF WATERS

This Large Print Book carries the
Seal of Approval of N.A.V.H.

GATHERING OF WATERS

BERNICE L. MCFADDEN

THORNDIKE PRESS
A part of Gale, Cengage Learning

GALE
CENGAGE Learning·

Detroit • New York • San Francisco • New Haven, Conn • Waterville, Maine • London

GALE
CENGAGE Learning·

Copyright © 2012 by Bernice L. McFadden.
Thorndike Press, a part of Gale, Cengage Learning.

Thorndike Press® Large Print African-American.
The text of this Large Print edition is unabridged.
Other aspects of the book may vary from the original edition.
Set in 16 pt. Plantin.

LIBRARY OF CONGRESS CATALOGING-IN-PUBLICATION DATA

McFadden, Bernice L.
    Gathering of waters / by Bernice L. McFadden. — Large print ed.
      p. cm. — (Thorndike Press large print African-American)
    ISBN-13: 978-1-4104-4582-7 (hardcover)
    ISBN-10: 1-4104-4582-8 (hardcover)
    1. Mississippi—Fiction. 2. African Americans—Crimes against—Mississippi—Fiction. 3. African American families—Fiction. 4. Mississippi—Race relations—Fiction. 5. Large type books. I. Title.
PS3563.C3622G38 2012
813'.54—dc23   2012001561

Published in 2012 by arrangement with Akashic Books, Ltd.

Printed in Mexico
1 2 3 4 5 6 7 16 15 14 13 12

For Richard May
& Lula Mae Hilson-May

You are souls immortal, spirits free, blest and eternal; ye are not matter; ye are not bodies; matter is your servant, not you the servant of matter.

— Swami Vivekananda, 1893

PART ONE

CHAPTER ONE

I am Money. Money Mississippi.

I have had many selves and have been many things. My beginning was not a conception, but the result of a growing, stretching, and expanding, which took place over thousands of years.

I have been figments of imaginations, shadows and sudden movements seen out of the corner of your eye. I have been dewdrops, falling stars, silence, flowers, and snails.

For a time I lived as a beating heart, another life found me swimming upstream toward a home nestled in my memory. Once I was a language that died. I have been sunlight, snowdrifts, and sweet babies' breath. But today, however, for you and for this story, I am Money. Money Mississippi.

I do not know for whom or what I was named. Perhaps I was christened for a farmer's beloved mule or a child's favorite pet; I suspect, though, that my name was derived from a dream deferred, because as a town, I have been impoverished for most of my existence.

You know, before white men came with their smiles, Bibles, guns, and disease, this place that I am was inhabited by Native men. Choctaw Indians. It was the Choctaw who gave the state its name: Mississippi — which means *many gathering of waters.* The white men fancied the name, but not the Indians, and so slaughtered them and replaced them with Africans, who as you know were turned into slaves to drive the white man's ego, whim, and industry.

But what you may not know and what the colonists, genociders, and slave owners certainly did not know is this: Both the Native man and the African believed in animism, which is the idea that souls inhabit all objects, living things, and even phenomena. When objects are destroyed and bodies perish, the souls flit off in search of a new home. Some souls bring along memories, baggage if you will, that they are unwilling or unable to relieve themselves of. Oftentimes these memories manifest in humans as déjà vu. Other times and in many other life-forms and so-called inanimate objects, these displays have been labeled as curious, bizarre, absurd, and deadly.

You may have read in the news about the feline having all the characteristics of a dog, the primate who walked upright from the day he was born until the day he died, of men trapped in female hosts and vice versa, the woman who woke one morning to find that she had grown a tail, the baby boy who emerged from his mother's womb flanked not in skin but scales, the man who grew to the towering heights of a tree, rivers overflowing their banks, monster waves wiping away whole cities, twisters gobbling up entire neighborhoods, relentlessly falling snow blanketing towns like volcano ash.

These are all memories of previous existences.

Listen, if you choose to believe nothing else that transpires here, believe this: your body does not have a soul; your soul has a body, and souls never, ever die.

To my memory, I have never been human, which probably explains my fascination with your kind. Admittedly, I am guilty of a very long and desperate infatuation with a family that I followed for decades. In hindsight, I believe that I was drawn to the beautifully tragic heartbrokenness of their lives, and so for years remained with them, helplessly tethered, like a mare to a post.

Their story begins not with the tragedy of '55 but long before that, with the arrival of the first problem, which came draped in crinoline and silk; carrying a pink parasol in one hand and a Bible in the other.

CHAPTER TWO

In 1900, the Violet Construction Company purchased a tract of land on the south bank of the Tallahatchie River and dug up the bones of the Choctaw Indians and the Africans. They tore from their roots black-eyed Susans, Cherokee roses, and Virginia creepers, and removed quite a number of magnolia and tupelo saplings. They did all of this to make room for forty three-story clapboard homes complete with indoor plumbing, grand verandas, and widow's walks. A road was laid to accommodate horse and buggies and the rare motorcar. The cobblestone sidewalks were lined with gas street lanterns and the street itself was christened Candle.

Oak floors, chandeliers, wainscoting, and brass hardware dazzled potential buyers who came to view those homes that looked over the prettiest part of the river. The people walked through the spacious rooms

15

holding their chins and sighing approvingly in their throats as they admired the fine woodwork and custom details.

The homes sold very quickly.

With the creation of Candle Street came jobs for laundresses, maids, and cooks, which brought in more people to the area — darker people.

So in 1915, the Violet Construction Company purchased a second tract of land, this time on the north shore of the river.

The north shore tract was cleared of most of the ancient, towering long-leaf pines whose thick canopy had deprived the land of sun, which turned the earth hard, dry, and as uneven as a washboard. Running vines speckled with yellow thorns coiled around trees, rocks, and the carcasses of animals and people who had stopped, dropped, and died there. The Violet Construction Company removed all of it and used the cheapest grade of pinewood to erect thirty modest-sized homes that did not have indoor plumbing, widow's walks, or verandas. At night the Negroes had to depend on the light of the moon to guide them along the rocky, cratered footpath. And if there was no moonlight — well, God help them.

The Violet Construction Company named

16

the street Baxter's Road, but since only Negroes occupied those homes, both black and white alike began to refer to the little community on the north shore as Nigger Row.

The church, funded by the Negro community, was built in 1921. The residents of Candle Street gifted their dark, wooly-haired neighbors a small crate of Bibles and a proper crucifix set with a blond-haired, blue-eyed Jesus molded from plaster of paris and nailed resolutely to its center. The Negroes did not have a man of the cloth living amongst them, so sent out word that they were in search of a suitable cleric to lead their flock.

As fate would have it, Reverend August Hilson and his family had recently been displaced by the race riots that erupted in Tulsa, Oklahoma. The Negroes who managed to avoid being shot down in the streets like dogs, or burned to a crisp as they slept in their beds, packed up what they could and fled Tulsa.

For weeks, August and his family lived like nomads, wandering from one town to the next until they wandered all the way to Greenwood, Mississippi. There, August learned that his services were in dire need, "Just down the road," the bearer of the news advised, "in Money."

August Hilson and his family took posses-
sion of a home on Nigger Row on a cool
November day. The photographer from the
local newspaper came to capture the auspi-
cious occasion. The family posed on the
porch. August was seated in a mahogany
chair cushioned in red velvet. The long, dark
fingers of his right hand curled around his
favorite Bible. His left hand rested on the
intricately carved lion's head which looked
out at the photographer from its post at the
top of the armrest. His wife, a peanut-
colored, petite, full-bosomed woman named
Doll, stood dutifully at his right side with
her left hand on his shoulder, her right hand
wrapped around the long neck of her beloved pink parasol. The children — a daughter named Hemmingway and a son named
Paris — were stationed to the left of their
father, arms still at their sides.

It was the first time any of them had ever
been photographed, and even though they
were practically bursting with glee, their
expressions were painfully somber and their
postures were as stiff as stone.

From beneath the dark blanket that covered both photographer and camera, the

photographer counted off: *Three . . . two . . . one . . .*

The bulb exploded, expelling a puff of white smoke. A cheer went up from the small crowd that had gathered to watch the spectacle, and the Hilson family officially began their new lives.

Days later, when August was presented with a framed copy of the newspaper article, he took it into the drawing room where the light was brightest. There, August stood for many minutes gazing wondrously at the grainy picture. He thought they all looked like wax figures — well, all except Doll, who had the faintest wisp of a smile resting on her lips.

August was too modest a man to hang the framed article on the wall for every visitor to see, so stored it away on a bookshelf. Every once in a while, when he was home alone, he would remove the framed treasure and ogle the picture.

Over the years, the clipping yellowed and curled behind its protective glass, and the photo began to distort and fade. Sometimes when August peered at it, Doll seemed to be sneering; other times, she bared her teeth like a badger. August blamed the changes in the picture on figments of his imagination, poor light, and aging eyes; he had a bagful

19

of explanations to explain it away. The final straw, however, came when he looked at the picture one day and saw that Doll's middle and index fingers on both hands were crossed; August could not for the life of him decide if the gesture had been made in hope of good luck or for exclusion from a promise.

He tossed the memento in the river, but it was too late — his fate was already sealed.

CHAPTER THREE

Doll was the love of August's life, but she was also a thief.

Back in Tulsa, she had closed her arms around the shoulders of an elderly parishioner and expertly procured a shiny, dark plume from the woman's brand-new Easter hat.

She was a bandit — stealing her daughter's prized silk hair ribbons and all of her son's blue marbles. When she saw the children crying over the loss, it filled her with giddy pleasure.

Before the children came, Doll had even stolen her husband from his first wife. It wasn't her fault — the spirit of a dead whore had taken root in Doll's body on the very day she was born.

Doll's mother, Coraline, was six months pregnant with her second child when Doll, who was five at the time, looked up from the bowl of shelled peas and asked, "Mama, how was I when I was a baby?"

Coraline was slicing carrots for stew. She stopped, raised the back of her hand to her sweaty forehead, and swiped at a damp braid of hair. The question unearthed a memory and a smile.

"You come into this world screaming holy murder, and didn't stop until you were a month old. Like to drive me outta my mind. It was your daddy — God rest his soul — who stopped me from throwing you down the well." Coraline laughed and swiped at the braid a second time.

Doll raised her hand and stroked the taut skin beneath her chin. "Maybe *you* the one shoulda gone down the well," she said.

The knife slipped from Coraline's hand and clattered to the table and her mouth dropped open in surprise.

The statement was horrible — yes — but the voice behind the statement was terrifying. Esther Gold, Esther the whore — dead and buried for half a decade, and now come back in her daughter, in her Doll? Coraline blinked with disbelief.

Esther the whore had been a fixture in Tulsa, and could be spotted, day in and day out, wrapped around light poles, beckoning men with a wiggle of her finger, hissing like a snake: "Pssst, come here, I got something

22

that'll make it all better."

She had been a beauty once, bright-skinned and thick-legged, with a curtain of hair that stretched all the way down to her waist.

Esther.

Too pretty for any woman to want as a friend. So beautiful, men didn't think about loving her; they only fantasized about melting away between her creamy thighs.

Poor Esther.

The men she welcomed into her heart and into her bed should have worshipped the ground she walked on — and they did for a while — but eventually her beauty felt like a hot spotlight and their confidence faded away beneath the luminous beam. They questioned her loyalty and themselves.

Why she want me?

The answers always fell short of what they needed, which was a scaffold of assuredness sturdy enough to bear their egos. Esther replied, "I love you, ain't that enough?"

They said it was, but it wasn't and they didn't know why. So the men beat her for loving them.

They beat the goodness and the sweetness out of her. They beat her into the streets, into back alleys, down into the dirt, into the gutter, onto her knees, her back, and then they climbed on top and emptied their miseries inside her.

Esther.

The voice was unmistakable, but Coraline had to be sure, so she said, "What you say, gal?" And Doll repeated herself in the same whiskey-and-cigarette scarred voice.

Coraline rounded the table, caught Doll by the collar of her dress, and dragged her out the house and down the road to the old woman called Sadie, who had herbs and potions that would deal with a tramp soul like Esther.

"Uh-hmmm," Sadie grunted as she used her thumb and forefinger to stretch Doll's eyelids open. After peering in the right eye and then the left, Sadie rocked back on her heels and nodded with confidence.

"Yeah, she in there all right." Sadie shook her head pitifully. "Sorry for this, but it make sense now, all that hollering she done when she come into this world."

Coraline nodded her head in agreement and then folded her arms around her swollen belly and began to sway.

"Sit down, Coraline, before you fall over," Sadie warned. "You remember how she die?"

"Who?"

"That old whore."

Coraline eased herself into a nearby chair, dropped her head into her hands, and forced her mind to look back. "I think she was stabbed to death."

"So she died by the blade? You sure? You gotta be sure now."

Coraline pounded her fists against her temples. "Yeah, someone cut her throat." Her eyes swung to her daughter's complacent expression and back to Sadie's well-lined face. "You gonna be able to pull that whore outta my child?"

Sadie chewed on her ragged bottom lip. "Every tramp soul is different. Some stronger than others." She glanced at Doll who was looking up at the ceiling, her eyes intent on something. Sadie slowly followed her line of vision, but there was nothing to see but wooden planks and cobwebs. She brought her palms together in a resounding clap.

Both Doll and Coraline jumped at the sound.

"Look at me, child," Sadie gently demanded. She leaned over and brought her nose within millimeters of Doll's, caught her roughly by the chin, and said, "Esther, Esther, we gonna get you outta this child and send you straight to hell where you belong!"

Doll held the old woman's gaze, skinned

back her lips, and spat, "And I'ma take you with me, witch!"

Coraline shrieked and Sadie lurched back.

"Ooh, Esther," Sadie sneered as she walked a wide circle around Doll. "When I'm through with you, you gonna be sorry you were ever born!" And then to Coraline, "You go along home now let me do what I need to do."

The old woman moved to the door and pulled it open. A sheath of daylight sliced across the floor and the multicolored glass canisters and jugs shelved along the back wall.

"Come back for her in the morning."

Coraline scrambled out the door.

When Coraline returned the next day, Sadie handed her a sealed jar filled with murky water.

"Esther in here?" Coraline asked, holding the jar at arm's length.

"Her spirit," Sadie said.

"Well, what am I supposed to do with it?"

"Dig a hole as deep as you can, pour the water in it, and then cover it up."

Coraline eyed the jar for a minute and then looked over at Doll who was sitting at the table, nibbling on a biscuit.

"She look well enough," Coraline said to

Sadie, and then cocked her head and addressed Doll: "How you feelin'?"

Doll glanced up from her biscuit. Her lips were covered in crumbs. "Fine, ma'am," she responded in her five-year-old voice.

"Come on now, you can take that biscuit to go."

Doll jumped out the chair and moved across the floor toward her mother. Coraline's eyebrows arched with concern — Doll's legs were crisscrossed with bright red switch marks.

"Y-you beat her?"

Sadie narrowed her eyes and grabbed hold of her slim hipbones. "I ain't beat *her* — I beat the whore inside her."

Doll moved to her mother's side and took her hand. Mother and daughter's fingers entwined and a familiarity surged through Coraline's veins.

"Remember now," Sadie warned, "that hole gotta be deep. Dig all the way to China if you have to."

Dearest, you cannot bury a soul! Souls are light, darkness, and air. Coraline found this out the hard way, when five years after she buried the jar and thought that she had rid her daughter and the world of Esther and malice, Esther reappeared, stronger and

27

more spiteful than ever.

Coraline had spent most of the day in the yard, boiling, scrubbing, and hanging sheets. Doll helped some, but she was clumsy and easily distracted. Three separate times she'd lost her grip on a freshly washed sheet, and all of the hard work went sloshing down to the dusty ground.

Coraline sucked her teeth in anger. "Girl, you causing me double work!" She sent Doll off with a vicious wave of her hand. "Take your brother with you."

"I'm sorry, Mama."

"That you are," Coraline hissed as she crumpled the sheet into a ball and dropped it back into the pot of hot, soapy water.

Hours later, Coraline entered the house in search of salve to apply to her chafed red hands. Her mood was low, but soared when she heard the joyous laughter of her children seeping from her bedroom. A favorite hiding place for brother and sister was beneath Coraline's double-sized bed.

Her sore hands forgotten, a mischievous smile lit on Coraline's lips when she tiptoed into the room, raised one corner of the mattress, and peered down through the jungle of coiled bedsprings.

"Gotcha!"

But she was the one who got a surprise.

Doll's bloomers were down at her ankles and the hem of her dress was gathered around her neck. Conner, her five-year-old brother, had an index and middle finger inside of Doll's pussy.

The same two fingers he slipped into his mouth at night and sucked until dawn. The two fingers he stroked Coraline's cheek with and used to spoon up and eat cake batter.

Coraline went deaf and dumb with rage. She would have preferred blindness — death even — to block out the vision before her.

When Conner saw the shocked and angry look on his mother's face, he withdrew his fingers and they came out slick with Doll's nectar.

Coraline snapped, toppling the mattress and the bed onto its side, then pounced on Doll and wrapped her hands around the child's throat.

Conner ran from the house and into the road, where he stood frantically waving his arms and shrieking, "Help! Help!"

A neighbor, who had been sitting on his porch rolling tobacco, stood up and called to the boy, "What's wrong?"

"My mama is killing my sister!" Conner screamed back before sticking his fingers in his mouth.

Yes, *those* two fingers.

CHAPTER FOUR

Sadie was dead, and it was the best for everyone really, because her particular type of magic would have been useless in that situation.

So, Coraline took Doll to the reverend.

"You can have her," Coraline said, and shoved Doll roughly toward him. "Ain't no good in her, only Esther, and she's all bad."

The reverend's eyes swung wildly between Coraline and her sobbing daughter.

"Sister Coraline, I can't —"

Coraline backed away. "Nah, nah, Reverend, you gotta take her or I'ma kill her for sure," she warned as she raised her right palm to the sky. "I swear to God, I will kill this child and then the blood ain't gonna just be on my hands, your hands gonna be red too."

August Hilson gently took hold of Doll's arm and she flinched in pain. That's when he noticed the black and blue bruises.

"My Lord," he whispered in horror, "did you beat this child?"

Coraline was already walking away. She turned her head slightly and slung, "No, Reverend. I didn't beat Doll; I beat the whore inside of her."

August led Doll into the house and guided her to the sofa. "Sit here," he said, and then disappeared into the kitchen.

His wife Ann was standing over the sink, stuffing seasoned rice into the belly of a raw chicken. "Who was that at the door?" she queried without turning around to look at him.

"Ann."

The seriousness in her husband's voice was heart-stopping. Ann slowly turned to face him. August was gray.

"What is it? What's wrong?"

In the living room, Doll could hear August's hushed explanation, which was followed by Ann's shrill "She did *what?*"

In a moment, Ann was at Doll's side, cradling her against her bosom.

"My sweet, sweet Jesus," she murmured. "What kind of mother would do this to her own flesh and blood?"

August shook his head in dismay. "Coraline is hot now. Maybe in a day or two —"

Ann's head snapped up. "In a day or two *what?* Don't tell me you're thinking about sending this poor child back to that woman?"

August was thinking exactly that.

"Oh, I won't have it, August. Next time might be the last time for this little girl. Doll is staying right here with us."

August and Ann had a child of their own named Vesta. A six-year-old with a lisp and tender ways. At the dinner table that night, Vesta shoveled forkfuls of steamed rice and baked chicken into her mouth, all the while keeping her eyes glued to Doll.

After dinner, Ann dressed Doll in one of her half-slips. "You'll wear this until I can find you a decent nightgown," Ann said, before tucking the girl into bed alongside Vesta.

She read them a story, and planted soft kisses on each of their foreheads. The "I love you" Ann shared before closing the bedroom door was big enough for both girls.

In the darkness Vesta whispered, "I been praying for a sister."

Doll's hand moved across the empty space between them, found Vesta's hand, and squeezed it. "Me too," she said.

■ ■ ■ ■

Doll slipped into the Hilson family as easily as a lost puzzle piece they didn't know was missing.

"See, I told you," Ann commented to August one day as she sat darning socks, "that Coraline was the crazy one. Doll's been nothing but a joy." She smiled to herself, knotted the stitch, and then used her teeth to sever the thread. "She's just the sweetest thing."

August, who was seated across the room sucking on his pipe and reading the newspaper, nodded in agreement.

A few years later, Ann's words — *She's just the sweetest thing* — would float back to August as he slid inside of Doll and exploded into a million points of light.

CHAPTER FIVE

When Doll turned fifteen years old, Ann baked a three-layer lemon cake to celebrate the occasion. The family sang happy birthday, then Doll blew out the candles and received as a gift her first pair of nylons. Three days later, Ann and August celebrated their tenth wedding anniversary. At the church, an excited Ann joined her husband at the pulpit with a folded square of paper clutched in her hand. The words on the paper were filled with love and exaltations — words that any husband would have been proud to hear his wife recite.

August was taken off guard.

"A speech?" he squawked in surprise. Ann nudged him gently aside and positioned herself squarely behind the podium.

Her eyes sailed over the black and brown faces that looked back at her before settling on the encouraging smiles of Doll and Vesta who were seated in the front pew with their hands folded daintily in their laps.

Ann cleared her throat, unfolded the paper, and began: "My husband and I have been married for ten wonderful years . . . When I was a child, I prayed that the Lord would send me a God-fearing man, a gentle and kind man, who would make a good husband and a good father . . ."

Ann stalled. She'd come across a word that she couldn't quite make out and so apologized for the interruption and raised the paper eye-level to try to figure out what she'd written. The paper slipped from her hand and floated down to the floor. Ann giggled with embarrassment and both she and August stooped to retrieve it — that's when Doll coughed.

It was a loud and boisterous cough that drew the attention of not only her surrogate parents, but quite a few church members as well. The husband and wife turned their heads in the girl's direction and Ann saw the thing she was not supposed to see.

Her eyes bulged and her smile stretched into a hard line. When she turned to August, his lips were forming the words: *Ann, please, please.*

Ann shot straight up.

The congregation shifted uncomfortably in their pews. Something had happened —

was happening — but they didn't know what. Ann backed away from August and his pleading eyes. When he reached for her, she looked down at his hand with such horror and disdain that one would have thought it belonged to the devil himself.

"No!" Ann screamed as she viciously slashed the air with the slip of paper.

Fear and confusion rippled through the church, people jumped to their feet, and in a moment, twenty concerned congregants, including Vesta, surrounded Ann.

"No, no, no!" Ann continued to bellow.

Doll remained in her pew, calmly watching Ann unravel.

Gloria Hardy was a beefy woman who had raised seven boys alone. She had been mother and father, protector and punisher, to those children. Her rise through the church ranks to become a deaconess was an accomplishment she was especially proud of.

It was Gloria who smashed through the circle of parishioners and grabbed Ann by the shoulders. Her intention was to force Ann down into a pew, before she tripped over her own feet and seriously hurt herself. But Ann, out of her mind with what she had seen, sunk her teeth into Gloria's aiding hand and Gloria forgot where she was and who she was and hauled off and punched Ann square in the nose.

By the time Gloria realized what she'd done, Ann's limp body was splayed out on the floor like a rag doll.

Back at the house, Ann was in bed, propped up on two pillows. Gloria had dressed Ann's swollen nose in gauze, lain a cool cloth over her head, and offered a thousand apologies before August was finally able to send her home.

When Ann finally regained consciousness, August was seated in a chair, which he had dragged in from the kitchen and set across the room against the wall.

Ann's eyes fluttered open. The room appeared to be draped in tissue and August looked like an apparition.

"Ann?"

She gently touched her bandaged nose and winced. She was grateful for the pain, the pain allowed her to know that she was not dead.

August stood and crept across the room. "Ann?" he called again, this time from the foot of the bed. Their eyes locked and Ann's stomach turned over. She thought she would be sick.

"August," she began in a surprisingly even

tone, "she didn't have any bloomers on."

August winced at her words.

"Don't tell me you didn't . . . notice."

He looked off to the window and muttered, "I didn't."

Ann smirked. "You've been my husband for ten years; you think I don't know when you're lying to me?"

"I'm not lying."

"Look at me."

August's gaze swept quickly across Ann's face and settled on the bare wall behind the bed.

"Are you fucking her?"

August gasped. She had never used that type of language, ever.

"Ann!"

He wasn't fucking Doll, but he had, in all fairness to you, dear reader, dreamed about fucking her.

You see, four months earlier, on Easter Sunday morning, August had seen Doll primping in the looking glass that hung on the wall in the bedroom she shared with Vesta. He happened to be walking by and the door was ajar, open just enough for him to glimpse Doll standing before the mirror straightening the bow in her hair and smoothing her hands down the pleats of her skirt. The girl pursed her lips and demurely batted her eyes at the vision that looked back at her, and August couldn't help but chuckle.

Doll went stiff, and August thought she sensed him standing there. But the moment seemed to come and go. Doll brushed a speck of lint from her collar and then brought her hand to her neck and started to stroke it.

August watched, mesmerized, until Ann called the family for breakfast.

In the church that day, on the pulpit, August made eye contact with everyone except Doll. Only when he uttered the first lines that would close the day's service did he chance a glance in her direction and was stunned to find the girl was not just looking at him — she was glowering.

An Easter egg hunt followed Sunday service. On the front lawn, the elders sat at picnic benches and younger members spread blankets. Children squealed with delight as they dashed from one discovery to the next, gathering dyed eggs. Doll was too old to participate in the hunt, but was more than happy to shadow Vesta in her pursuit.

The beautiful afternoon faded into a spectacular evening. The North Star was the first of its clan to make an appearance. Loons struck up a serenade and scores of fireflies pulsated through the night air. One by one, people gathered themselves to leave.

Good night, Reverend.

Happy Easter, Reverend.

August and Ann were seated at one of the picnic tables, holding hands and gazing up at the night sky.

"It was good day, wasn't it?" Ann said as she rested her head on her husband's shoulder.

"It was a glorious day."

Ann grinned.

"Where are the girls?"

Ann straightened up and looked around. "They're around here somewhere," she said. "I just saw them a moment ago."

"They're probably in the back. You wait here; I'll go and get them."

August rounded the church and spotted Vesta and Doll seated on the grass with their legs stretched out like matchsticks. A wicker basket heaped with colorful eggs rested between them. Doll's arm was extended over her head, the tip of her index finger trained at the sky.

"That there is the Big Dipper and the one over there is the Little Dipper . . ."

Vesta cooed with wonder.

"Okay, my little stargazers, it's time to head home," August announced upon his approach.

"Daddy, I think I got a splinter," Vesta said, and curled her right foot onto her lap.

"You did?" August eased down, took Vesta's foot into his hand, and examined the sole.

"Do you see it, Daddy?"

August shook his head. "It's too dark. Your mother will take a look at it when we get home."

"I looked and I didn't see no splinter," Doll murmured.

August patted the top of Vesta's foot. "Come on now, your mother's waiting."

Vesta rose to her feet, grabbed her shoes, and limped across the grass. August stood, brushed torn blades of grass from the knees of his trousers, and peered down at Doll.

"You too, let's go."

Doll demurely presented her hand and said, "Please help me up, Daddy August."

She had started calling him that just days after Coraline had abandoned her on his porch. Daddy August. She'd said it a million times, but never in that slithering tone. The hair on August's neck and arms spiked.

He took her hand and tugged, but Doll snatched it away and tumbled down to the ground, laughing. Her dress flew up, revealing smooth thighs and the pyramid-shaped mass of pubic hair between them.

August's eyes popped with surprise and he began stupidly stammering: "What . . . why . . ."

Doll's laughter turned raucous.

"Shut up," he whispered, looking fearfully over his shoulder. "Shut up and pull down your dress."

August wanted to slap her, kick her, and stomp her face until her mouth was swollen shut. The visions flashed recklessly through his mind, though he couldn't bring himself to do anything other than demand her silence.

"Shut up! Shut up!"

Finally, Doll stopped laughing.

After pulling her dress down and wiping the tears from her eyes, she extended her hand once again.

It was all August could do to keep from spitting on her. He stormed off, and Doll jumped to her feet and skipped along behind him.

The ride home was quiet and tense. In the carriage, Ann stared curiously at her husband's rigid back.

"You okay?"

"Fine."

In the house, she asked again and was met with the same stiff, cold response. Ann sighed, leaned over, pressed a soft kiss onto his cheek, and bid him goodnight.

An eerie quiet, as still as pond water, filled the house. August settled himself into his favorite chair, reached for the Bible on the side table, and pressed it against his heart. His mind was reeling, grappling with and trying to comprehend what he had seen, the way Doll had behaved.

Why in the world wasn't she wearing any undergarments? Should he tell Ann? Was the girl possessed? Could his own daughter be next?

August gave his head a violent shake, but the images and the questions held fast.

A door creaked open and he fixed his gaze expectantly on the narrow hallway that led to the bedrooms. Soon, Doll appeared.

August stiffened.

"Yes, Daddy August?" Doll yawned.

August couldn't speak.

"You called me?"

Had he?

August tightened his grip on the Bible.

Maybe he had.

"Come here, Doll." His tone was soft, but uneven.

The girl stumbled sleepily toward him.

Beneath the flickering glow of the oil lamp, she looked like the same sweet child he had welcomed into his home and raised as his own. Perhaps, he thought as he lowered the Bible down into his lap, he had imagined the spectacle.

After all, the day had been unusually warm. The sun had not been blistering — but hot enough to do damage to the senses. And he had been out without a hat. Not to mention his overindulgence of cured ham, buttered rolls, raspberry pie, and sweet tea. The combination could muddle the mind of any sane man. Couldn't it?

Of course it could, he told himself. Well, the proof was standing right next to him. He couldn't recall summoning Doll, but he must have, because there she was.

Embarrassed and ashamed, August hooked his pinky finger to Doll's and said, "Did you enjoy yourself today?"

She shot him a quizzical look. "Uhm, yes, Daddy August, I did."

"Good, good," August mumbled. "Now go on back to bed."

Over the days and weeks that followed, August tried to live his life as if that night had never happened and he had not seen that dark pyramid. But it haunted his waking and sleeping hours, and soon he found himself wondering about the treasure it hid. In his dreams, he did not have to wonder. In his dreams, Doll handed him the key and he would plunder and pilfer that pyramid until the roosters sang.

But outside of his dream state, he had not laid an unfatherly hand on the girl!

"I did not do this thing, Ann, you must believe me!" August wailed.

"Liar!" Ann screamed, then flew from the bed, pounced on August, and began pummeling him with her fists. "Youlowdownnogoodsonofabitch!"

August tried his best to fend her off, but Ann's rage overpowered him. He would not hit her back, he was not that type of man, so he crumpled to the floor and suffered the abuse.

Seemingly satisfied that she had brought her husband to tears, Ann fled from the room and down the hall in search of Doll. In the bedroom, Vesta was crouched down and pressed into a corner. When Ann burst in, Vesta shrieked with fear.

"Where is she?" Ann screeched.

The wide-eyed Vesta aimed a shaky finger toward the open window.

Outside, Ann circled the house, looked behind pecan trees, the outhouse, and underneath the porch.

Doll was nowhere to be found.

Ann marched from one house to the next, pounding on doors and shouting August's and Doll's transgressions into the stunned faces of those who dared answer.

"Your man of God! Your reverend is fucking that devil he brought into our home!"

August trailed Ann, offering apologies to the neighbors.

"Forgive her, she is not well. I think she has fever."

He pleaded: "Ann, please stop this nonsense. Come back home and let me get a doctor to see about you!"

She stooped down, gathered a fistful of pebbles, and pelted him. "Get away from me!"

Doubling back to the house, Ann went inside, shut and bolted the door.

August pounded on the door for three hours. He pounded until the side of his hand was raw as fresh meat, but Ann never allowed him reentry. He spent the night in the carriage, wrapped in the stinking, rough blanket he used to cover the horse.

The next morning, he was awakened by the sound of his wife's voice issuing demands: "Put that there. Careful now, don't break it."

47

August rolled back the blanket and peered out into the hazy light. Two men were hauling items from the house. One man August recognized as Ann's brother, Smith.

A chair, two side tables, crates filled with dishes, pots, pans, bed linens, drapes — all was loaded onto Smith's wagon.

Vesta shuffled out of the house and plopped down onto the top step of the porch. Her head was bowed, and August knew that her eyes were swimming with sadness.

His heart tugged.

Ann stepped out, pressed her fists into her hips, tilted her head toward the sky, and took a deep breath. She had never looked happier.

"Is this it?" Smith asked.

Ann nodded. "Yes, it's all I want." She looked down at Vesta. "We are going to be fine, you hear me? Just fine."

August would forever look back on that day, when his wife and child climbed onto that wagon and rolled out of his life, with great sadness and shame.

So you ask, why did he not leap from his hiding place, fall to his knees, and beg Ann to stay? While I know many things, there are many more that I do not know or understand. But I will speculate that in that moment, what was more important than his family or his reputation was his desire to bring his dreams to fruition.

After the wagon disappeared down the road, August went to sit on the porch steps. He sat until the sun was high in the sky and the flies took shelter in the shade. He sat until a rustling sound inside the house summoned his attention. He rose, stuffed his hands into the pockets of his trousers, and walked into the house. Doll was seated in his favorite chair, wearing nothing but the brown skin she was born with. Her legs were open and the dark pyramid was split in two, revealing a glittering pink star.

He was aware of the sound his boots made as he crossed the wooden floor. It was so loud he thought the entire world could hear him walking. When he reached her, he fell to his knees, grabbed hold of Doll's waist, buried his face in her stomach, and began to weep.

The girl stroked his hair and patiently waited for him to unload his sorrow.

Afterward, of course, there was the suckling of the pink star, the heat and pulse of it against his tongue, and Doll's moans, squeals, and writhing.

Poor August, a man of God, but still just

a man, and now a doomed man.

After the coupling, the bursting into wild brilliant lights, August declared that he would follow Doll to the ends of the earth. Sorry to say that the only place she would lead him was to hell — which turned out not to be the fiery underworld he preached about, but right here on top of the world with me.

Chapter Six

"He say his wife gone back home."

"Gone back home?"

"That's what he say."

"And nothing else?"

"Nothing else."

"He don't say why she gone back home? Sick relative maybe?"

"You need your ears cleaned out? I say all he say is she gone back home."

"Hmmmmm."

"Sound to me like she left him. Did she take the girls with her?"

"The girls? Ha, they ain't had but one between them."

"Awww yeah, I forgot about that. But that Doll been with them so long that she started to favor the younger one."

"Uh-huh, strange how that happens, ain't it?"

"I'll tell you what's strange!"

"What?"

"I took a casserole over to the house, 'cause you know menfolk don't know nothing about cooking, and —"

"But the girl, she old enough to cook."

"Well true, but I wasn't thinking 'bout —"

"What you make for him?"

"Shepherd's pie, but that ain't what I'm trying to get at."

"Sorry, you were saying?"

"I was standing at the screen door, knocking. I knocked a good long time and then I went on in —"

"You just walked on in the reverend's house?"

"I was knocking for a really long time. Yes, I just walked in and was gonna leave the plate in the kitchen, on the stove, but soon as I got my foot good in the door, there she was."

"She who?"

"Doll. Like she just dropped from the ceiling —"

"Like a spider?"

"Yep, but I ain't see no web."

"You know that child always been peculiar."

"Peculiar? Her mama claimed she was possessed by Esther."

"Esther Magnolia?"

"No, girl, Esther the whore."

"You don't say?"

"Yep! So anyway, Doll standing there in her slip, hair tussled, cheeks flushed —"

"In her slip? What she say?"

"She don't say nothing and so then I said, *I brought y'all a shepherd's pie,* and then I hear the reverend calling from the back room —"

"What? Wait . . . she was in her slip?"

"Now you're with me."

"Oh my God!"

"Mine and yours! And so I hear the reverend say, *Doll, Doll baby —*"

"Doll *baby?*"

"Yeah, *Doll baby, what you doing out there, bring that star back on in here.*"

"Star? What in the world?"

"After he call to her, she smiled, raised her hand, waved bye-bye, and turned and walked off."

"In her slip?"

"In her slip!"

"You think the reverend is laying that girl?"

"More like *she* laying *him.*"

"But sister, what star he talking about?"

"I only know about the ones up in the sky. Do you know of any others?"

"No, ma'am, I do not."

He would have married her without the talk, without the eyeballing, without the men of his congregation showing up unannounced to remind him what was proper and what wasn't.

"Look here," one man said, "we men, so we *understand*."

They did understand because they left their Bibles in their wagons, tucked their religion into the back pockets of their trousers, and placed a bottle of Jack Daniel's right at the center of the kitchen table.

Doll was in the bedroom, trying hard to contain the excitement the men walked into the house. Her skin was on fire and she began to spin to cool herself. When August came into the bedroom she was in the middle of the floor, whirling like a cyclone.

He caught her by the arm. "Here's a quarter. Go to the store and buy yourself something."

The men stood when Doll entered the room. She dusted them with her gaze, giggled, and then hurried out of the house. She was gone, but her scent hung as thick as mist in the air. The men inhaled it and swallowed.

"See, it's like this August . . ."

They passed the bottle between them.

". . . It just don't look right, you know, having this young girl living here with you . . . without another woman in the house."

". . . Yes, we know you raised her and Coraline certainly don't want her back . . ."

". . . She is a fine-looking girl. Fine!"

". . . Any man would be tempted to."

"— Being that you are a man first and a man of the cloth second."

". . . We don't want you to be tempted to do what a lesser man would . . ."

". . . And the women clucking like hens about what's going on here, and you know . . ."

". . . That make them look at us funny, and we got enough problems already and don't need our women accusing us of messing around, so you either."

". . . Put Doll outta your house or divorce your first wife and take Doll as your second!"

August took their advice, and within the month the two were betrothed. It was a scandal, of course, and he lost 20 percent of his congregation. Some of the female neighbors stopped talking to him and would just as soon spit fire on Doll than address her as Mrs. Hilson.

"There's only one Mrs. Hilson and that is Ann Hilson!"

When word reached Coraline, who had moved down to Sperry, she huffed and said, "I ain't a bit surprised." But she was curious and begged a ride from a man who was sweet on her. "Carry me into Tulsa, please, I gotta see about some business."

"On a Sunday?"

Coraline gave the man a hard look.

"Aw'ight, come on."

She slipped in the last pew and pulled her hat low over her forehead. On the pulpit August waved the good book until the sleeves of his robe flapped and billowed. He jumped and ballyhooed, stomped and spoke in tongues, and encouraged his congregation to do the same.

Coraline chose to reveal herself just as the collection was being taken up. Head held high, she strolled right up the center aisle, deftly ignoring the whispers and finger-pointing.

"Morning, Reverend."

"Morning, Sister Coraline. Nice to see you again."

Coraline turned and looked at Doll.

"Doll," she said.

Doll returned Coraline's query with a polite and respectful, "Mama."

Coraline looked at August. "It's true? You done gone and married the girl?"

August shuffled, tried to smile, but it emerged as a frown. "Yes, ma'am, I did."

Coraline stripped her teeth. "Okay," she said with a toss of her head. "I just had to hear it from your mouth."

"Well, now you've heard it."

"Yes, I have."

August didn't know what possessed him, but he raised his Bible into the air and cried, "What God has brought together, let no man pull asunder!"

Coraline cocked her head to one side and said, "What the good book say about what *Esther* has brought together?"

CHAPTER SEVEN

Less than a year after they were married, Doll gave birth to a girl who they named Hemmingway. A boy followed three years later, and they named him Paris.

Doll didn't make a good wife or a good mother.

She did not allow her children to call her Mama or Mommy — "You call me Dolly. *Doll-lee!*"

She did not cuddle, tend to runny noses, or wrap their necks with woolen scarves to protect them from the cold. She may have fawned and fussed in public — but in the privacy of their home Doll avoided the children with the same vigor she used to evade housework.

For the most part, her days were spent lounging in her slip, sipping sweet tea, listening to George Tory and Skip Blake albums on the phonograph. The only reason she even attended church service was because she enjoyed the arresting effect her presence had on the congregation.

Besides all of that, one of the only other things she enjoyed doing was making johnnycakes. Even those people who did not like her had to admit that Doll's johnnycakes were the best they'd ever tasted. Light, fluffy, heaven-on-your-tongue, melt-in-your-mouth type of good. So good it almost made her behavior acceptable.

Almost.

One evening, August bid Doll and the children goodbye and set off with two ministers to host a midnight revival.

"I'll be back by sunup," he said as he mounted his horse.

Doll shrugged, "Okay."

In the darkest part of the night, Hemmingway awoke to Paris's wailing. She climbed from her bed, went to his crib, and stuck her finger in his diaper. It was wet.

Hemmingway walked confidently down the hallway toward her parents' bedroom. Unlike most children, she was not afraid of the dark. Upon reaching the bedroom door, she rapped softly on it while calling, "Dolly? Dolly?"

There was no answer, so Hemmingway turned the knob and pushed.

"Dolly?"

The room was cast in shadows. She could see the gray silhouette of her mother's body stretched out on the bed.

"Dolly, Paris is wet and I think he's hungry too."

The silhouette shifted and the bedsheets rustled. A voice the girl had never heard before said, "Hemmingway, is that you? Come in here, sweetness."

Can a voice have fingers? That one did. Icy fingers that closed around Hemmingway's young heart.

The darkness shifted and the silhouette sat up. "Come here," it cackled.

Hemmingway backed out of the room, ran down the hallway and into her bedroom. She dragged the painted wooden rocking horse across the floor and pushed it up against the closed door.

Paris was screaming by then, but his sister barely noticed above the sound of her galloping heart. The baby screamed himself hoarse and finally fell asleep. Hemmingway remained awake, watching the door and listening for the voice with the icy fingers. She did not know when sleep stole her away, but she would always remember the dream that followed of her and Paris running for their lives through a dark, lush forest. On their heels was a wolf wearing the face of their mother.

The next morning Hemmingway woke to find Paris gone. Fearing that the wolf in her dreams had taken him, she leapt from the bed and crept out of the room. The air in the house was soaked with the scent of bacon, eggs, grits, and johnnycakes. She could hear her father's voice chiming merrily in the kitchen.

Doll was seated at the table, nursing Paris. When she looked up and saw Hemmingway standing in the doorway, her face turned bright with pleasure.

"Morning, darling, how did you sleep?"

"Hey, baby," August smiled.

Hemmingway watched them. Not sure yet if this was part of her nightmare, she remained in the doorway.

"Oh, we're not speaking this morning?" Doll sang.

August frowned. "What's wrong with you?"

The girl took a tentative step into the bright light that streamed through the kitchen windows. "Daddy?"

"Yes?"

Hemmingway flew into him and nuzzled her nose deep into his neck. He smelled like night air, liniment, and scorched cedar chips.

He was real. It was not a dream.

August patted Hemmingway's back and shot Doll a questioning look. Doll shrugged her shoulders and pried Paris's lips from her nipple.

"Baby," August crooned as he tried to peel Hemmingway off of him, "what in the world is wrong with you today?"

"Oh, August, stop babying that girl," Doll admonished. "You've got her spoiled rotten!" Doll rose from her seat, propped Paris on her hip, and addressed Hemmingway. "I made you some oatmeal. It's in the bowl over there on the stove. Come on now, let go of your father."

Hemmingway held fast.

"Sweetheart, what's wrong?" August gently pushed Hemmingway off of him and began to examine her. He took her face into his hands, glided his fingers down her arms. "Are you hurt?"

"Who would hurt her, August?" Doll snapped. "I'll tell you what's wrong with her, she likes too much attention, that's what!"

Hemmingway slipped from her father's lap.

"August, you need to wash up and get to

bed. You look whipped."

He nodded dutifully, but his eyes were still resting on Hemmingway's face. "You're okay, right?"

She glanced at Doll, who was glowering at her. "Yes, Daddy, I'm fine," she whispered.

"Good." August gave his daughter a tender pat on her head and walked out of the kitchen.

"Take care of them dishes when you're done," Doll ordered as she followed August out.

Hemmingway didn't move to retrieve the bowl of hot cereal until the slapping sound of Doll's house slippers had faded away. At the table, she spooned up a large helping of the cereal and brought it to her open mouth.

Good thing she smelled the turpentine before she ate it, or this story might have ended here.

CHAPTER EIGHT

Cole Robert Payne lived in one of those nice houses on Candle Street. He was a big man, with dark wavy hair and bright green eyes. He had a wife, who was small, meek, and sickly. They had no children.

Before Cole came to Candle Street, before he married Melinda, and before he took ownership of the only store here that welcomed both blacks and whites, he was a sharecropper's son in a town not too far from me known as Sidon.

As a boy, Cole lived with his family on the edge of a thin line that separated rich from poor and black from white. This line was as significant as the one that separates the sky from the sea. It was this line that Cole stepped unwittingly across.

The Payne's neighbors were a black family named Johnson. They had four sons and a little girl named Sissy.

Sissy was a dark-eyed, lanky, smiling child

with a space between her two front teeth. Cole and Sissy had been born months apart. Cole's mother Catherine helped pull Sissy into the world, and when Catherine fell ill and was unable to nurse Cole, Sissy's mother Ethel stepped in and did it for her.

They were friends, these two families from opposite sides of the line.

Sissy and Cole were two peas in a pod from the time they could walk. When they turned five years old, Sissy stole a hatpin from her mother, and beneath a tree in the Paynes' front yard, she used it to prick Cole's finger and then hers. They mashed the open wounds together and declared their eternal allegiance to one another.

How could they have known that this promise would turn into love?

Before I move forward, I think it's only right that I educate you about spring.

Spring has always had a female essence and will forever be a noxious season, choking the air with her scent, having her way with clouds — shaping them into all manner of impractical things. Even the crickets do not escape spring's demands. To satisfy her wishes, from April through June they strum nothing but Francisco Tárrega's "Recuerdos de la Alhambra."

Spring is lovely, but she is also a trickster! She can make you forget that you are the wrong color, old, ugly, or fat, and fills your head with foolish possibilities. She impresses upon your heart affections for people who will have nothing to offer in return.

Her showers wash away the gray blotches of winter and everything may *appear* new. But be aware, there is nothing new, there is only the old shrouded in spring's bright floral dress.

Over time, Cole and Sissy grew up and apart, their two-peas-in-a-pod friendship dwindling down to just a passing *hi.*

That changed one day when Cole strode up the road toward home. He was moving slow, his long arms swinging languidly at his sides like loose ropes. He was thinking about the fly ball he'd caught and the whipping he was sure to suffer for slipping away to play baseball instead of finishing his chores.

Sissy was sitting on the wooden railed fence that encircled a wide field chock-full of colorful wild flowers. She was gnawing on a cob of corn when she spotted him.

"Hey," she sang.

"Hey, Sissy," Cole called back without slowing his gait.

"Your mama made some johnnycakes. I

66

had myself two. They taste like a little piece of heaven."

Her voice carried notes he had never heard before. The sound caught him by surprise and stopped him dead in his tracks. He turned around.

"You want some company?"

Sissy shrugged her shoulders indifferently and started on another row of kernels.

Cole trotted over and hoisted himself up onto the fence. Sissy noticed the muscles in his arm rippling with the effort and her stomach did a little somersault.

He looked out over the blanket of purple, pink, and orange blossoms and waited for something in him to stir. "What you looking at?" he asked.

"Nothing and everything."

"Well, why you sitting here?"

"I was here for the peace and quiet, but I guess now that *you're* here, that's all done with," she chuckled.

Cole laughed, leaned over, and bumped his shoulder against hers. "Fun-nee!"

Sissy hushed him and with a nod of her head, directed his attention to the sky. "Look," she whispered.

For five full minutes they sat silently watching the sun slowly bleed into the horizon. When the miracle was over, Sissy let off a long, satisfied sigh and flung the cob across the field.

Cole watched it sail through the air and disappear into the blanket of flowers. When he turned to look at her, Sissy was wearing an expression that was so serious, his heart skipped a beat. "What?'

Her response was a broad, corn kernel–filled grin. They both exploded with laughter.

Eyes leaking and sides splitting, the two friends fell into one another with merriment. Sissy doubled over and would have ended facedown on the ground if not for Cole's quick reaction and strong forearm.

"Grab on!"

Sissy hooked her fingers around his arm and was tugged back to safety. "Thanks."

Her fingers were still wrapped around his forearm when the first twinkling star appeared.

The sound of an approaching wagon shattered the magic and her hand dropped away. She hopped down to the ground. "I guess I should be getting home."

"I'll walk ya."

"Okay."

Spring.

That very night, Sissy began to think about

Cole in the way she had only ever thought about Mac Gosling, a colored boy she was sweet on who lived two miles away. She found that the butterflies that invaded her stomach whenever she saw Mac also took flight when her mind stumbled on Cole. And it started stumbling on Cole often, so much so that if her mind had had ankles, those ankles would have had bruises.

In Cole's mind, Sissy suddenly became a fixture, similar to the crucifix that hung over his parents' marriage bed. He yearned for her, and rather than trying to quell the desire, he fed it by visiting the fence and running his hands over the slab of wood where the two of them had sat.

He so desperately wanted to own something that had touched her, or that she had touched, that he spent an hour in the field hunting for the corncob. He didn't find it, and when he went home his clothes were saturated with the scent of flowers. His father coughed his annoyance and asked Cole if he'd abandoned the baseball field for a funeral home.

Once, when Cole thought he was alone in the house, he tried to reclaim the moment by imitating the laughter Sissy had expelled on that afternoon, and his mother walked in on him in the midst of a girlishly shrill

69

giggle. She tapped him on the shoulder, and when the startled Cole swung around, he came face to face with his mother's perplexed gaze.

"Boy," she calmly asked, "are you losin' your mind?"

Cole blinked wildly. Yes, he believed he was.

Spring.

CHAPTER NINE

How they got away with it for as long as they did was a mystery to me. By the time they were found out, it was way past spring and weeks beyond their first awkward kiss. There had been hundreds of kisses by the time summer swaggered in, bringing with her days upon days of sweltering heat.

It was summer's heat that drove Sissy's father, Edgar, off the road into the sparse shade of a pecan tree. If it hadn't been so hot and Edgar had just kept walking up the road toward home, Sissy and Cole's affair might have gone undetected for years.

I'll just sit here a minute and rest, Edgar told himself as he dragged the blue and white kerchief across his damp brow. Weariness crept over him and he braced his back against the bark of the tree, cocked the brim of his hat over his eyes, and soon fell fast asleep.

Further up the road, Cole was sitting in

the crook of a gnarly tree limb, working the tip of his mother's kitchen knife into the bark.

"What you doing up there?"

He looked down to find Sissy squinting at him. Tiny balls of perspiration covered her face, and when she tilted her head, the sun ignited the orbs, gracing her with an undeniable shimmer.

Cole grinned.

With the handle of the knife clenched securely between his teeth, Cole began to make his descent with the assuredness and agility of a monkey. He hit the ground with a large thud.

The lovers glanced warily around before leaning in and stealing a kiss. They crossed the road, climbed over the fence, and moved through the blanket of flowers to the bald spot of earth which had been scuffed talcum-soft by their lovemaking.

She tasted like syrup.

He tasted like his mama's johnnycakes.

She felt like butter.

He felt like an iron poker warmed in kindling.

An earshot away Edgar woke from his nap, stretched his arms over his head, and released a great yawn. His gaze swept over the field and stopped on a cluster of swaying flowers.

That's odd, he thought before licking his finger and testing the air to find that it was still as death. He rose to his feet and set off to investigate the phenomenon.

As Edgar moved closer, he heard laughter. He knew that laughter, playful, teasing — lovers' laughter. He stopped walking.

Out here in the open?

He couldn't help but smile at the couple's brazen outrageousness.

"Well," he muttered aloud as he turned around to leave, "I was young once too."

His intention was to head home, but his mind kept wandering back to the flowers and the laughter.

Who are they?

It was easy to imagine their heat, their complete surrender to one another — but try as he might, he could not imagine their faces. Curiosity got the better of him and he decided to hang around a little while longer, just to see what they looked like.

He returned to the shade to wait. He couldn't imagine that the couple would go on for much longer — not in that heat.

Cole rolled off Sissy and onto his back. His penis slumped lazily across his thigh. Sissy reached for his hand, pulled it to her mouth, and slipped his fingers between her lips. Cole began to giggle.

They lay there in that field as if it were their own home and the ground beneath them their bed.

"I gotta go."

"I know." He turned onto his side and gazed deep into her eyes. "I'm already missing you," he breathed, and then leaned in and pressed a gentle kiss against her lips. "Let's run away together and get married."

Sissy laughed. "Who would marry us? A white boy and his nigger mistress?" She laughed again, but this time the notes were flat.

Cole's eyes dimmed. "You ain't no nigger. I hate that word."

"Come on," she said brightly, "help me up."

From where Edgar sat, it seemed as if Cole had emerged from the soil and unfurled like some exotic flower. An exotic, *naked* flower.

Edgar wasn't yet over the first shock when he was rattled by the second. His heart dropped down into his gut when the brown-skinned girl appeared.

Edgar stood up and took a few steps forward. "What colored girl . . . ?" he mumbled to himself, and then realized it was his own daughter.

He didn't even know he was running until the tunnel of wind he created tore his hat from his head.

Sissy was still trying to get her arm into the sleeve of her dress when she looked up and saw her father charging toward them.

"Sissy!"

Cole spun around and jumped protectively in front of her. His green eyes flashed, and Edgar stalled.

Edgar knew he could beat Cole with one hand, if he had to. He was a full foot taller and twenty pounds heavier, but there were shadows swimming in his blind anger, and the line that separated black from white coiled into noose; imagined or not, Edgar could feel the rough rope fibers brushing against his neck.

Edgar took a very deep breath.

"Sissy, come here."

"You don't have to go with him, Sissy!" Cole barked.

"She's my child, Cole, you done enough. Lemme take her home." Edgar's tone was replete with disappointment and defeat.

Sissy dropped her head. She wiggled the remaining length of arm through the sleeve and stepped shamefully away from Cole.

"Daddy I —"

Edgar shook his head. He didn't want to hear any of it.

What could she have said to him to make what she had done — had been doing — all right? That she was sorry? That she was — *God forbid* — in love with Cole Payne? No words she could speak would ever be powerful enough to change the fact that Cole was white and she was black and this was Mississippi, U.S. of A.

Edgar's long, brown face was etched with sadness and when Sissy finally looked at him, it broke her heart to see that she had broken his.

She would have gladly taken a beating — a million beatings — if it would place the happy back onto her father's face.

"Let's go home," Edgar said before turning and walking away. Sissy followed, weeping into her hands.

Edgar never uttered a word about the discovery to his wife or to God. He didn't have to; Sissy never wanted to see her father look at her in that way again, and so the next time she saw Cole Payne — she *didn't see* Cole Payne. And whenever Cole called down to her from his waiting place in the tree, Sissy held her head straight and hastened her pace.

It went on like that for some weeks, until Cole finally understood that it was over. He didn't accept it though, and remained awake at night trying to figure out ways he could get Sissy back. The boy was so distraught, so out of his mind with longing, that he took to lying in the field beneath the afternoon sun dressed in nothing but his drawers. Why? Well, to get dark, of course!

He stupidly thought that if he was a darker shade of white, Sissy's father might accept him. But all he got for his effort was sunburn and a slight case of sun poisoning.

Cole's parents didn't know what was wrong with him. His father told him that he'd take him out to the shed and beat the sense back into him if he didn't shape up and stop acting crazy.

Turns out, Cole didn't need a beating from his father, all he needed was to see Sissy strolling hand-in-hand with Mac Gosling, and just like that his broken heart turned to dust. You know, dust barely has any feeling at all.

A few months after the sighting, Sissy and Mac Gosling married. Throughout the better part of her marriage, and certainly for as long as her father breathed air, Sissy did not dare allow her mind to run on Cole Payne. But I know that when Edgar passed away, and he lay serene and silent in his casket, unable to dish out penalty or retribution, Sissy *did* allow her mind to wander back to that amazing spring and loved-filled summer, and the memories raised a smile amidst her tears.

Cole, well, he let go of the idea of having Sissy as his wife, but try as he might, he couldn't push the memories out of reach. Sometimes nostalgia got the best of him and he'd try to recreate the magic they had. It was despicable and embarrassing to watch him usher one white girl after the other to that fence.

He told them to laugh and say: *Your mama made johnnycakes; they taste like a little piece of heaven.*

The girls, they did as he asked.

Anything for Cole Payne.

"Your mama made johnnycakes; they taste like a little piece heaven."

Again.

"Your mama made johnnycakes; they taste like a little piece of heaven."

Again!

"Your mama made johnnycakes; they taste like a little piece of heaven!"

The melody was never quite right and the girls always cried when they saw the regret shining in his eyes.

CHAPTER TEN

Arthur Thompson owned the land that both Cole and Sissy's family sharecropped. For years, Cole had witnessed Arthur come by once a month to collect the rent and part of the crop. He was a short man with red cheeks and sparkly blue eyes. He always counted the rent money aloud. Afterward, he'd swipe the bills across the leg of his trousers, before folding the stash in half and shoving it into his pocket. Cole took that as a slight. It was as if the sweat his family put into earning the money had soiled the cash, rendering it too dirty for Arthur's pocket.

Other than that, Arthur seemed like a decent man. Oftentimes he'd sit on the porch with Cole's parents, telling stories and crude jokes.

Arthur had two sons and a daughter. The girl, Melinda, sometimes rode out with her father on collection day. She would sit up front with her bare feet sticking out the window. Sometimes she wore shorts, other times soft skirts that fluttered in the breeze.

She always stayed in the truck, and Cole's mother, Barbara, thought that it was rude how the girl never came out to speak to them.

"Would your daughter care for some lemonade?" Barbara ventured one day.

"Aww, she's all right. She got a Coke in there if she get thirsty."

"She don't ever get out the truck. Is she shy?"

Arthur's bushy eyebrows rose. "Shy ain't the word. If she could live her life inside her bedroom, she would," he whispered. "If I didn't bring her out on my rounds with me, the child would never get any fresh air or sun."

Cole's mother huffed. "Well, that can't be good. What she do in the house all day?"

"Read."

"Oh."

On one particular day, when Melinda felt her father was dawdling way too long, she angrily honked the horn. Arthur sighed, rose, and patted his money-filled pockets.

"I guess that means it's time to go."

"Aw right now," Arthur said as he rose. "I'll see y'all next month." Halfway down the walkway, he spun around. "I think I

81

need to use your facilities before I head off."

Cole's father pointed toward the side of the house. "It's just 'round back."

Cole waited until Arthur was out of sight before he announced that he was going to introduce himself to Arthur Thompson's impolite daughter.

Barbara giggled. "Yes, you should. Be nice though."

At the truck, Cole stuck his face through the open driver's-side window. Melinda had her head buried in a book, and so when he yelped, "Hey, how you doing?" it startled her, and the book fell from her hands and tumbled down to the floor. "I'm Cole Payne," he announced thrusting his hand at her.

The flustered Melinda said nothing. Her eyes searched frantically for her father.

"And you're Melinda, right?"

The young woman shook her head no and then yes.

Cole's hand hung in the air between them. "This is where we shake and you say something back," he laughed.

"Yes, of course." Melinda hesitantly extended her hand. "I'm Melinda Thompson. Pleased to meet you."

Cole grabbed hold of her hand and pumped it enthusiastically. "Nice to meetcha, Melinda Thompson!" He noticed that she had her father's brilliant blue eyes and curly blond hair. The square chin and thin-as-a-line nose, Cole assumed she'd inherited from her mother.

"Oh, uhm . . . yes . . . you too. I mean, me too . . . I mean . . ."

Cole released her hand and sniffed the air. "It smells nice in here. Is that you?"

Melinda blushed. "It's the perfumed talc I'm wearing."

Cole made a face. "Talc? What's that?"

Melinda leaned over, retrieved her book from the floor, and placed it in her lap. "Powder."

"Powder?" Cole scratched his chin. "What kinda powder? Like gunpowder?"

Melinda stammered. "No-n—"

Cole waved his hand at her. "I'm just pulling your leg, Melinda," he laughed.

She cautiously joined in on his laughter. "Oh, of course."

"Well, it was nice to finally meet you and see you." He fashioned his thumb and index finger into a gun, aimed at her, winked, and clucked his tongue. "I thought you were just a pair of pretty feet."

Melinda's cheeks glowed.

"See ya." And with that, Cole thumped the top of the truck and trotted off.

Melinda watched him until her father's bloated belly floated into view.

"What you staring at so hard?" Arthur asked as he climbed into the truck.

"Nothing."

Arthur turned the ignition and popped the clutch. The truck jerked forward and then settled into an easy roll.

Back at home, Cole's smiling face swam circles in Melinda's mind. She looked down at her hand and could swear she saw the imprints of his fingers on her skin. When she knelt to say her prayers before bed, she asked the Lord to keep Cole Payne safe.

The next month, Melinda once again accompanied her father on his collection rounds. Same as always, she rode with her feet dangling out of the truck window. But now those pretty toes were adorned with pink nail polish.

Arthur parked the truck on the road, in the shade. He turned off the ignition and before he could reach for the door handle, Melinda was out of the truck.

A look of astonishment perched on his face. "What are you doing?"

"Coming along."

Barbara Payne met them at the door.

"Afternoon," she said, and then directly

to Melinda: "Hello, so nice to finally see you . . . err . . . meet you. Please come in."

They followed her into the house. Melinda looked around at the modest surroundings. The sitting room wasn't much bigger than her own bedroom and everything — couch, chair, woven throw rug — seemed to be a variation of the color brown.

"Please, have a seat," Mrs. Payne said as she hurried to the couch and fluffed the one limp pillow that graced it. "John is out back fiddling with something." Her speech was hurried. "We weren't expecting you this early. I'll go out and get him."

Father and daughter sat down. Melinda wondered if she was in the very spot where Cole sat. She closed her eyes and conjured up the vision.

"Melinda?" Arthur's voice was cold. "What in the world are you doing?"

Her eyes snapped open. "Nothing."

Barbara reappeared. "He's coming now. Can I get you all something to drink?"

Arthur shook his head. "No thanks, I gotta get back home soon. Got family coming in from Miami."

"Miami," Barbara repeated in a dreamy voice, as if Arthur had said, *I got family coming in from the moon.*

Melinda said, "I'd like something to drink,

Mrs. Payne."

"You do?" Arthur uttered.

"Yeah."

Barbara scurried off. When she returned with a tall glass of lemonade, her husband was handing over the rent money.

Arthur counted the money, swiped it across the leg of his trousers, folded it, and stuffed it into his pocket.

Melinda's eyes darted from one corner to the next. Where was Cole? She attempted to stretch the time by taking small sips of lemonade. If she did it right, she could make that drink last for more than half an hour.

Barbara noticed how little Melinda was drinking. "Is it too tart, dear?"

"No, ma'am," Melinda muttered without looking at her.

Arthur scratched his large belly. "Come on, Melinda, we gotta go."

The daughter rolled her eyes and handed Barbara the glass. "Thank you."

"You're welcome, sweetheart. I do hope we'll see you again."

Melinda offered Barbara a small, disappointed smile. She'd painted her toes, dusted her body with an extra layer of the perfumed talc, and even washed her hair with her mother's special — off-limits to her — shampoo. So much work and risk and

86

not even a Cole sighting. Melinda was deflated.

She knew she wouldn't be able to survive thirty more days without seeing Cole Payne. And besides, school was due to start in another two weeks, and she would no longer be able to make the collection rounds with her father. Which of course meant that she would probably never see Cole Payne again.

Melinda couldn't ask either of her brothers to drive her out — there would be too many questions asked. She didn't have any friends to speak of and the local buses didn't go that far away.

Melinda looked down at her feet. She could walk, but in the heat she was sure she'd melt away in under an hour.

Her mind ticked.

There was her bicycle. A brand-new Schwinn she'd gotten as a birthday gift and had only ridden twice.

She smiled.

The following weekend, Melinda announced that she was going to the library. Her mother, Connie, was in the kitchen instructing their maid in the art of stringing a rump roast.

"Okay, see you later," Connie sang without

taking her eyes off the raw meat.

Melinda rolled the bicycle down the driveway and onto the street. She mounted it and began to peddle. The bicycle wobbled wildly through the first few rotations. Finding her balance, Melinda shot like a rocket through the center of town and past the Sidon library, out toward the rural area. The breeze raised her hair off her neck and forehead, and Melinda had the sense that she was flying.

Cole was outside and shirtless, tossing a ball back and forth with his younger brother, when Melinda rolled into the yard.

He blinked unbelievingly. "Melinda?"

She offered a breathless, "Yeah, hi."

The sight of his bare sun-kissed torso set her skin on fire.

Cole strolled over to a nearby tree, snatched his shirt from a high limb, and shrugged it on. "What are you doing out here?"

Melinda hadn't thought about the questions and so she had no prepared answers. "Just riding." She laughed a little too loudly.

"All the way out here?"

She bounced her head up and down like a seal. She felt giddy, like her head was filled with soap bubbles.

Cole's eyes moved to the road and then back to Melinda's flushed face.

"Do your parents know you're out here?"

"It's okay," she sputtered, "I told them I was going to the library."

Melinda Thompson hadn't crossed Cole's mind since he last saw her. But he could see now, as she stood there quivering with excitement, that she had done little else *but* think about him.

"Oh, so you missed me, huh?" Cole teased smugly.

Melinda blushed.

"Come on," he said as he wrapped his hands around the handlebars and guided the bike to the house.

"Who's that?" Cole's little brother asked.

"This here is Melinda Thompson. Now go find something to do elsewhere."

The brother threw his mitt angrily to the ground and stomped off.

Melinda and Cole sat down on the porch steps. Cole did most of the talking. He talked about baseball, comic books, and farming. Every so often he would lightly touch her arm when making a point, and it was all Melinda could do to keep herself from falling to pieces with pleasure.

Inside, Barbara eavesdropped and fretted from behind the curtained window. She couldn't imagine that the girl's parents knew she was out there keeping time with Cole Payne — the son of a sharecropper. And if they found out, what would the implications be? Would Arthur kick them off his land? Raise their rent? Ask for a larger portion of the crop? Barbara's head began to hurt.

"That girl," she muttered to the air, "is going to bring us a whole heap of problems."

When Melinda finally left, Barbara breathed a sigh of relief. Cole sauntered into the house and tossed a "Hey, Ma" at her before throwing himself down into a kitchen chair.

"What that Thompson girl want?"

Cole grinned. "Me, I s'pose."

Barbara bristled at his arrogance. "She outta your league, boy, and we don't need no trouble from her daddy, ya hear?"

Cole heard her, but that didn't matter. Melinda was prime for the slaughter; he just had to decide where and when.

CHAPTER ELEVEN

Melinda arrived home just in time for dinner.

"My," Connie exclaimed. "You been gone all day. You must have read a dozen books!"

Melinda floated up the staircase, down the hall, and into her bedroom. If the world had come to an end right then and there, Melinda wouldn't have complained. She had had the most perfect day of her life and the destruction of heaven and earth couldn't take it away from her.

Was she happy? Happy was too small a word to describe what she was feeling.

Melinda flung herself onto her bed and screamed with glee into the pillow.

Three days was as long as Melinda's desires allowed her. Any day beyond that and she was sure her heart would burst from her chest, mount her bicycle, and ride itself out to visit Cole Payne.

"I'm off to the library, Mom!" Melinda shouted from the driveway.

Barbara was sweeping the porch when Melinda rolled into the yard. Barbara's heart sunk, but she still managed to force a bright smile.

"Well, hello there, Melinda," Barbara said as she folded her arms across her stomach.

"Hello, Mrs. Payne. How are you?"

"I'm well, and yourself?"

"Fine, ma'am." Melinda's eyes swung to the house. "Is Cole home?"

Barbara's hands reached for her elbows and she dug her fingernails into the tender skin.

"No, he's not."

"Well, where is he?"

Barbara blinked at the girl's forwardness. She didn't want to respond and even considered grabbing her up and swatting her across her behind to teach her some manners, but instead she said, "He's in the fields, working."

"Where's that?"

Barbara bit down on her lip and nodded back in the direction Melinda had come. "Down the road a bit on the left," she said through gritted teeth. "But like I said, he's working."

Melinda thought about it for a moment. "Do you mind if I wait?"

Barbara wanted to scream: *No, go back home and find yourself one of your own kind and leave my Cole be!*

"Not at all," she breathed.

Inside, over cookies and lemonade, Barbara found the girl to be, well, charming, and her earlier steeliness began to soften.

"These cookies are really, really good, Mrs. Payne."

"Thank you. I baked them myself."

"Really?"

"Yep. Doesn't your mom bake?"

Melinda shook her head no. "Sara does all of the cooking and baking in our house."

"Sara?"

"Our maid."

"Oh." Barbara refilled Melinda's glass. "So, do you know how to bake?"

Again, Melinda shook her head no.

Even as she made the offer, Barbara couldn't quite understand why she was doing it. "If you'd like, one day we can bake some cookies together. I'll show you how."

Melinda lit up like a glowworm. "Really?"

"Sure."

There were other things the girl didn't know how to do: iron, wash clothes, clean house. Barbara pitied her.

The back door soon opened and the Payne men spilled in for their afternoon meal.

"Oh Lawd," Barbara exclaimed. "I haven't even made lunch."

They filed into the kitchen and their mouths dropped open when they saw Melinda sitting at the table.

The youngest boy said, "What she doing here?"

"Mind your manners," Barbara chastised. "Melinda has come for a visit."

John uttered a low "Hello."

Cole said, "Hey, girl, how ya been?"

If Melinda were a balloon she would have floated straight up to the ceiling and popped. "Fine. You?"

"Great! So what's for lunch?"

Melinda helped Barbara prepare sandwiches and she alone stirred the sugar and lemon into the iced tea, poured it into the mason jars, and set them before each of the Payne men.

After lunch, she followed Cole to the back door and stood watching him slip his feet into his work boots.

"You gonna be around when I get back?" he asked.

Melinda looked at the sky. The sun was heading west. The library closed at four and she needed to be home soon after that. "What time will that be?"

" 'Bout seven or so."

"No, I have to get home, but I can come back on Sunday."

Cole clucked his tongue. "That's tomorrow, ain't it?"

Sunday morning, the house was filled with the aroma of fried fish and grits.

Sara knocked softly on Melinda's door. "Miss, you up? Breakfast ready. Church today."

Melinda groaned.

The door eased open and Sara's round, brown face peeked in. "Miss?"

"I don't feel so good."

"You sick?"

"My stomach hurts."

Sara's eyes swam with sympathy. "Poor thing. I'll get you some Bromo-Seltzer."

After the rest of the family headed off to church, Sara began chopping up the boiled potatoes and eggs for tater salad. Upstairs, Melinda slipped on a pair of shorts and a white blouse and brushed her hair into a tail, which she piled high atop her head and secured with a barrette.

Carrying her tennis shoes, she slipped quietly down the stairs and out the front door. The loud click of the lock brought Sara into the foyer calling, "Is someone there?"

Under an overcast sky, Cole Payne took Melinda Thompson by the hand and guided her through the field of flowers to the place where he had passionately taken Sissy Johnson and then, later, other women.

"This my most favorite place in the world," he said as he removed his shoes and shrugged off his shirt.

Melinda was unsure what it was she was supposed to do at that juncture, so she just watched.

When Cole reached for the zipper of his pants, Melinda turned her head away. "What are you doing?"

"Freeing myself," Cole laughed. "You should try it."

Melinda trembled with excitement. "I-I can't," she whispered.

"Sure you can. It's easy."

She kept her back to him. "No, no, I can't."

"Why, you on your period or something?"

Melinda's entire face turned red with

shame. What did Cole Payne know about periods? "No!"

Cole chuckled. "Turn around."

Melinda turned slowly around to find a completely naked Cole, stretched out on his back with one leg folded over the other. She was relieved to see that his genitals were hidden behind his thighs.

"Come here," he said.

Her heart raced as she inched timidly toward him. Cole patted the earth. "Here. Lay here next to me."

She positioned herself alongside his body. Melinda felt dizzy being so close to him, so close to his nakedness.

"Why don't you take your blouse off?"

The idea was mind-numbing, and everything she had been taught told her that she should not do what Cole Payne was asking her to do. But it was too late; she was lost the moment she laid eyes on him.

Melinda sat up, quickly unbuttoned her blouse, pulled it off, and tossed it aside. She lay back down next to him and used her hands to cover her brassiere-clad breasts.

"No, don't do that," Cole whispered as he gently removed her hands. He reached over and freed first the right breast and then the left. Melinda closed her eyes and began to pant.

Cole rolled her hard nipples between his fingers until Melinda went limp.

The entry was slow, painful, and sweet. As he rode her, he conjured a picture of Sissy in his mind. When his seed burst from his shaft, scalding and thick, it was Sissy's name that Cole screamed, not Melinda's.

CHAPTER TWELVE

Just a month after he had taken Melinda out into the field, she came to him weeping.

"I think I'm pregnant."

Even though her tears were real and flowing, and the distress in her voice was clear, Cole still asked, "You joking?"

"No, Cole."

He kicked a stone, fumbled with the lobe of his left ear, and mumbled, "You know anyone who can get rid of it?"

Melinda gasped, "Cole!"

"You're not thinking about keeping it, are you?"

Melinda shrugged.

"You can't be thinking that, Melinda. You can't. Your father will kill me!"

And then she said the words that changed Cole Payne's life forever: "Well, not if we get married."

The statement was filled with so much hope and longing that it made Cole feel sick.

"Married?"

Cole always assumed that he would marry for love and not circumstance. But he supposed he could do a lot worse than Melinda, who was monied, educated, and weak in the knees for him.

His female prospects were many — but all cut from the same poor cloth as he was. Cole could have stomached a life of poverty with Sissy by his side, but without her, it seemed a senseless and ridiculous choice.

"I guess," he uttered, "marriage would be the right thing to do."

They told his parents first, and then hers.

Arthur, who had never laid a hand on any of his children, grabbed Melinda roughly by the shoulders and shook her until his wife cried out for him to stop.

The wedding was a small affair, held in the Thompson's home. Cole's mother could have slashed her wrists with the envy she felt upon stepping into that house.

For a wedding gift, Barbara gave them a piece of framed needlepoint which read, *Happy Family,* in bright pink, green, and blue thread.

Arthur and Connie's gift was obviously much more extravagant: a deed to land, a store, and a house located miles away from

Sidon, here with me, Money Mississippi.

Years later, as Cole Payne sat reading the evening paper on the veranda of his home on Candle Street, he heard the melody he'd mourned for decades.

"Morning, Mr. Payne." A Negro woman smiled up at him as she walked toward the rear of the house. Cole peered over the top of the newspaper. The woman looked familiar, but he couldn't place her.

As if reading his thoughts she said, "I'm Reverend Hilson's wife."

Cole folded the paper. "Oh," he grunted, and then tilted his chin toward the wicker basket she carried. "What you got there?"

"I made Ms. Melinda some johnnycakes," Doll sang.

"Is that right?" Cole offered.

"You know, my johnnycakes taste like a little piece of heaven," Doll offered with a laugh as she rounded the corner of the house.

CHAPTER THIRTEEN

The Paynes' housekeeper was a dark, robust, mute woman named Caress. She clapped her hands with joy when she saw Doll's face on the opposite side of the glass window and quickly flung open the door.

Doll said, "Hello, how you today?"

Caress bobbed her head and grinned. She grabbed Doll by the wrist and dragged her over to the stove and pointed frantically at the shiny silver soup pot. Doll raised the lid and sniffed.

"Oh, that smells real good, Caress, real good." Doll rubbed her belly for emphasis.

Caress's grin stretched. She cast a quick look over her shoulder and then pressed her index finger against her black lips.

Doll nodded and winked.

Caress picked up a spoon, dipped it into the pot, and scooped up a luscious peach wedge, turned bronze by the mixture of sugar, cinnamon, and orange juice.

Doll pursed her lips, blew cool air over the cooked fruit, and then flicked her tongue against the sweet flesh. "Mmmmm," she sounded before closing her entire mouth over the spoon. "Is this for preserves?"

Caress nodded.

"That's real good, Caress, best I've ever tasted."

Caress dropped the spoon into the sink, grabbed Doll's hand, and pumped it until Doll thought her arm would fall from its socket.

"Okay now, okay," Doll laughed. "Is Miss Melinda in the drawing room?"

Caress shook her head no, made a sad face, and then pointed to the ceiling.

"She in the bed?"

Caress nodded yes, and swept her hand upward.

"She want me to come up?"

Caress nodded again.

Doll walked into the dining room, through the parlor, down a long hall, and up the broad and winding staircase. On the top floor she made her way down a carpeted corridor, at the end of which was the Paynes' bedroom. She knocked on the closed door.

A thin voice replied, "Come in."

Doll had been to that room twice before,

but the size of it and the lovely furniture always took her breath away. The bedroom was decidedly female. Cole had moved out a year earlier and taken up residence down the hall in the spare bedroom. "I just think you'd be more comfortable," he'd said as Caress carted clothing from the main bedroom into the spare.

The drapes were open and the sun spilled in, in great waves of yellow light. Doll took a moment to survey the space. With each visit, Doll had made it her business to commit every detail of the room to memory, and so it was very easy for her to spot any new additions. On that day, Doll's eyes fell on a small crimson vase adorned with white egrets.

"That vase is new," Doll said as she floated into the room.

"Well hello to you too," Melinda scoffed weakly.

"Oh, hello, Miss Melinda. I hear you're ailing."

Doll waltzed over to the nightstand and set the basket of johnnycakes down, alongside the vase. The day was warm, but the fireplace was lit and Melinda was wrapped in a pewter-colored goose-down comforter.

"Miss Melinda, you're shaking like a leaf." Doll retrieved the woolen throw from the foot of the bed and spread it gently over Melinda's already heavily covered body. "Is that better?"

"Yes, thank you."

I need to interrupt here for a minute and let you know that soon after Cole and Melinda married, she miscarried the baby. Back then, she was strong and positive and thought for sure that the next one would stick — but it didn't. And the same fate held true for the following three pregnancies.

After the last miscarriage, Melinda developed a severe case of anemia, along with a host of ailments that flourish when you humans are sad or depressed.

She'd been to see dozens of doctors who had prescribed her just as many medicines and tonics — but nothing seemed to help. Not a surprise, because even I know that you can't cure unhappiness with a pill — even though your kind continues to try.

Melinda gave Doll a pitiful look and sputtered, "I've gone and caught pneumonia."

Doll's eyes bulged. "Pneumonia? Oh my sweet Jesus."

"I'm hot to the touch, but I feel like there's ice running through my veins."

"How long have you had this fever, Miss Melinda?"

"Two, maybe three days now."

Doll pressed her hands over her heart. "Well that ain't good, not good at all."

Melinda started hacking and coughed up a glob of green phlegm, which she leaned over and spat into her chamber pot.

"May I?" Doll asked.

Melinda nodded, even though she had no idea what she was giving the woman permission to do.

Doll rolled back the blankets exposing Melinda's petite frame, which was so frail it didn't even fill the thin nightgown she wore. When Doll reached for the hem of the gown, Melinda's hands began to flail.

"It's okay, Miss Melinda," Doll assured. She took hold of the hem and rolled the material up to Melinda's belly button.

Melinda's thin, sun-deprived calves, thighs, and pink bloomers glared up accusingly at Doll.

"What are you doing?" Melinda whispered.

Doll gently pressed her hands against Melinda's belly and closed her eyes.

Melinda watched, and rationalized why she was letting the Negro woman touch her beneath her gown. She supposed desperation was a major factor because she was truly sick and tired of being sick and tired. If Doll had suggested that the sacrifice of a cow or fowl would rid her of her illnesses, and bring her husband back into their marriage bed, Melinda would have agreed — wholeheartedly.

Hell, she had been poked, prodded, and prescribed medicine by some of the best doctors in Mississippi, and what good had it done her? So, really, what harm could the caring hands of a reverend's wife present?

Doll's eyes fluttered open. "The fever is low in your belly, that's a good thing. I know what to do." Doll turned and rushed from the room.

Melinda rolled her gown back down and pulled the covers over her body.

When Doll returned, Caress was with her, holding a bowl. Melinda smelled the onions before she saw them.

"Miss Melinda, where do you keep your nylons?"

"Nylons?"

"Yes, ma'am. Trust me."

Melinda coughed. "Caress, you know where they are."

Doll used her bare hands to shovel the sliced onions into the feet of the nylons and then slipped them onto Melinda's feet.

"Caress, hand me a towel so we don't spoil these beautiful sheets," Doll said.

"And what will all this do?" Melinda asked.

"It's going to drag that nasty fever right out of you."

"It stinks."

"And it's going to get worse. But you're going to feel a whole lot better."

Doll went to the wicker basket filled with johnnycakes, plucked one from the dozen, and presented it to Melinda. "Try to eat little something."

Melinda shook her head. "I can't keep nothing down."

"Well," Doll sighed, as she dropped the cake back into the basket, "I'll just leave them down in the kitchen and when you're ready, they'll be there."

Melinda rubbed her feet together and squirmed at the sensation. "Uh-God, Doll, I don't know if I can take it."

"Yes, ma'am, you can and you will. I guarantee that the fever will be gone by the end of the day."

Doll's gaze traveled across the room and to the window. Her hand floated to her neck.

Melinda thought the woman had fallen into a trance. "Doll?"

"Hmmm," Doll sounded, turning her gaze back onto Melinda. "I'm sorry, I drift off sometimes." Her hand fell back down to her side. "Miss Melinda, I'm gonna have to be going now. I got to deliver some johnny-cakes to Ms. Fern and Mrs. Sawyer."

"Okay," Melinda mumbled. "Caress, get my purse —"

Doll shook her hand at Melinda. "Not a dime, Miss Melinda. Your recovery is all the payment I need."

"What about the johnnycakes?"

"On me."

"Are you sure?"

"Of course!" Doll beamed as she slipped the handle of the basket onto her wrist. "Now don't forget, you leave them nylons on until nightfall, okay?"

Melinda nodded in agreement.

Doll swept out of the room like a gale.

Sleep carried Melinda off to memories of easier times. When she awoke, the drapes were closed, night had fallen over the land, and the bedroom smelled god-awful. For a moment Melinda couldn't determine where the stench was coming from, and then she remembered the onions.

When she peeled the nylons off her feet, the onion slithers were black as tar. Disgusted, Melinda climbed out of the bed and tossed the foul-smelling nylons into the dying fire. At that moment she became keenly aware of three things as she stood watching them burn away to smoke: 1) the bedroom already reeked, so throwing the onions into the flames probably wasn't the wisest thing to do; 2) she felt 50 percent better than she had before Doll's remedy; and 3) the crimson vase was gone.

CHAPTER FOURTEEN

Cole Payne leaned forward and gazed at himself in the bathroom mirror. He ran his tongue over his teeth, skinned back his lips, and examined his mouth. He dipped his hand into the jar of pomade and smoothed the clump of greasy, waxy substance over his mane of dark hair. After that, he headed to the bedroom to check on Melinda, who had felt well enough to get out of bed and sit in a chair. When he entered the room she was reading.

"How are you, darling?"

Melinda smiled. "Good." Her eyes lit on his hair and his crisp white shirt. She could smell cologne.

"Are you going someplace?"

Cole shook his head. "No, why?"

"You look like — well, nothing. You look very handsome today."

Cole crossed the room and pecked her on the cheek. "I do it all for you, sweetheart."

That was a lie. The extra care he'd taken with himself on that day, and on all of the Tuesdays that would follow, was for Doll Hilson. You see, Tuesday was the day she delivered her basket of johnnycakes.

Cole stationed himself on the veranda and watched the street for Doll. When he spotted her, he became as excited as a schoolboy on Christmas day.

"Morning, Mr. Payne," Doll greeted with a soft smile.

"Morning, Doll." Cole's response was outrageously loud and cheerful.

As soon as she disappeared around the side of the house, Cole snatched open the French doors, sprinted across the parlor, down the hall, and slammed into the kitchen just as Caress was opening the back door.

Both Doll and Caress were startled by his sudden and rowdy arrival, and the women exchanged perplexed glances.

Cole glanced stupidly around the kitchen before his eyes fell on the pot of coffee simmering on the burner. "I believe I will have some more coffee," he said.

Caress nodded, reached up and removed a cup and saucer from the cabinet, and then ambled over to the stove.

"So, how is your husband doing?"

Doll's eyes popped with surprise. Cole Payne had never said more than two words to her.

"*My* husband?" Doll spouted with astonishment.

Cole laughed. "Well, Caress is a widow, so I must be talking about *your* husband."

Caress set the cup and saucer down before Cole and filled the cup with coffee.

"He's fine, thank you. I will let him know that you asked about him."

Caress spooned three heaps of sugar into Cole's coffee and added a dab of milk.

"Doll, would you like a cup of coffee?"

Cole could have said, *Doll, would you like to kiss me?* for the dense and uncomfortable silence that followed.

Caress's head did a slow and comical spin. When it stopped, her eyes were wide and her mouth was an open, gaping hole.

"Sir?" Doll said.

"Coffee. Would you like some?"

"Well, uhm . . . I don't . . ." Doll stammered.

"Caress," Cole demanded in a casual tone, "pour Doll a cup of coffee."

Caress didn't move.

"Have you gone deaf as well?" Cole snapped.

Caress stuck out her bottom lip and

folded her arms defiantly across her breasts.

"Caress!" Cole bellowed, and brought his fist down onto the table. The teaspoon rattled to the floor and coffee swilled over the rim of his cup.

Caress scrambled to the cupboard. Cole composed himself, bent over, and retrieved the spoon from the floor. When he was upright again, he saw that Doll was still standing at the door.

"Please," he said, as he rose, rounded the table, and pulled a chair out. "Sit down."

Doll's hand floated to her neck and began to stroke it. "Thank you, Mr. Payne," she purred.

While Doll was being served coffee at the Payne residence, her daughter Hemmingway, nearly fifteen years old, was headed toward the grocery store that Cole owned. Utterly unaware that the innocent sway of her hips and perfect onion-shaped backside bouncing beneath her skirt was causing a stir amongst the men she passed.

They — the men, that is — wouldn't dare admire Hemmingway in the manner they desired: wide-eyed and frothing at the mouth. She was, after all, the reverend's daughter — so they glanced, glimpsed, and peeked, like shy two-year-olds.

114

There was one amongst them, however, who took every opportunity available to make his desires known. His name was Mingo Bailey and he was infamous for his shameless pursuit of women and his triumphs over moist-eyed virgins.

"Pssst."

Hemmingway heard the offensive sound, but continued walking.

"Psssssssst!"

Annoyed, Hemmingway turned her head just enough to sling, "I look like a cat to you?"

Mingo stepped out from beneath the shade of a willow tree. "You *could* be *my* pretty kitty."

Hemmingway smirked, "I ain't looking to be some man's pet." She glanced down at the slip of paper she held which listed the items she was sent to purchase from the store.

Mingo fell into step behind her. His eyes lit on her bottom and then glided down her exposed legs, pausing at the dents behind her knees. Mingo began to salivate; he could spend a lifetime slurping pop from those tender spaces behind Hemmingway's knees.

"You better stop ignoring me, girl, or I'm gonna take this good stuff elsewhere."

He was tall and thin, but muscular. The

color of cedar, he walked with a bop because his left leg was longer than his right.

"Go on then," Hemmingway laughed as she stepped into the store.

Mingo lingered. He removed the cigarette he kept tucked behind his ear and rolled it thoughtfully between his fingers before replacing it.

When Hemmingway reappeared he fell into step beside her once again.

"Girl, you better start paying me some mind. How you 'spect you gonna get into heaven if you keep ignoring me the way you do?"

"I ain't your girl," Hemmingway snapped as she shifted the grocery bag from her left hip to her right. "And heaven ain't the place I'ma end up if I allow myself to deal with the likes of you!"

"Aw," Mingo sighed and reached for the bag, "lemme carry that for you."

Hemmingway stopped, turned to look him full in the face. "And what's that gonna cost me?"

"Cost?"

"Yeah. I hear Mingo Bailey don't do nothing for no one for free."

Mingo almost smiled. She had heard right.

"You're killing me, girl!" He grabbed his chest and roared with laughter. "I wouldn't take a red cent from you, baby." He reached for the bag. "I'd give you the world if I had it to give."

"For free?"

"Of course!"

Hemmingway handed him the bag.

They walked along in silence until they reached the bridge that connected Candle Street to Nigger Row.

After offering a curt thank you, Hemmingway reached for the bag, but Mingo held it away.

"I'll carry it all the way to your front door."

"So my daddy can tear my behind up for being with the likes of you? No thank you."

"What's so wrong with me?" Mingo asked, handing the bag over.

"I think you know," Hemmingway snorted, and walked off.

Mingo leaned into the splintered wood railing of the bridge and removed the cigarette from behind his ear. He pulled a long matchstick from the breast pocket of his shirt and swiped it against the heel of his shoe. By the time he brought the flame to the tip of the cigarette, Hemmingway was already on the north shore.

He took a long and thoughtful drag of the cigarette and wondered if Hemmingway

Hilson would be as feral a lover as her mother had been.

Doll was coming down the road from Cole Payne's house when she saw Hemmingway and Mingo. She ducked behind a tree and watched Mingo watching her daughter. Only after he flicked the cigarette butt into the river and walked away did she step from her hiding place. Doll started to follow him, but stopped when the reason for her pursuit suddenly vanished from her mind. You see, Doll thought she was suffering from lapses in memory. And I guess that would be the best way to explain away the periods in her life when Esther's will overpowered her own.

For Doll, childhood memories were choppy and gray. The months leading up to her marriage to August were cloudy. She could only recall bits and pieces of her pregnancies — although the labor and delivery of the children were vivid. Their escape from Tulsa in 1921 was quite clear in her mind. She remembered the night sky lit morning bright by the fires the white people set to the black-owned properties and the air filled with the scent of gunpowder and kerosene. Dead bodies scattered in the street.

Although she had been living here with

me for more than six years, she could not remember when they arrived, or the photo that had been taken of them on the front porch of their new home. The names and faces of the people here came and left from her mind just as quickly as the hours moved through the day. She suspected that her daughter didn't like her; the boy, however, seemed to worship the ground she walked on.

Even the moments before that moment, which found her standing in the middle of the road staring longingly at Mingo Bailey's retreating back, were hazy. What was bright in her mind was leaving home that morning headed to the Payne house to deliver johnnycakes. The next fresh memory was slipping behind the tree. She was sure that somewhere between the Payne house and the immediate moment she had consumed coffee, because it was swishing loudly in her stomach. She asked herself, *Why in the world would I drink coffee when I abhor the taste of it?*

Doll gave her head a hard shake, praying that the movement would retrieve the lost hours, but all it did was free a memory that Doll could only fathom as a dream.

In that dream, Mingo was headed to town with a pair of loaded dice in one pocket and two dollars in change in the other. His mind was so fixed on the money he intended to cheat his way into winning, that he barely noticed Doll waving at him from across the road.

"Mingo? Mingo Bailey?"

"Ma'am?"

"Can you help me to the bridge with these oranges? They're heavier than I expected."

Mingo looked toward the center of town and then back at Doll.

"Just to the bridge," she reiterated.

"Okay."

She hummed as they walked, and greeted passersby with bright, sunny hellos. When the humming stopped she raised her hand to her throat and began to stroke it.

At the bridge, Doll looked around and saw that there wasn't a soul in sight.

"Mingo?" she said in a voice far away from the one that had beckoned him from across the road.

"Yes, ma'am?"

"Would you like to have me?"

"Ma'am?"

"Have me. You know, the way you've had so many other women."

"Ma'am?"

"Fuck me. Do you want to fuck me, Mingo?"

He looked across the bridge toward Nig-ger Row. "I must be losing my goddamn mind," he muttered with a laugh.

"No, you're not," Doll assured, and pressed her hand against his crotch.

Beneath the bridge, on the Candle Street side, Doll became an animal; a spitting, scratching wildcat that Mingo struggled to gain control of. Above them, the sounds of shod feet, bicycles, and the clomping of hooves and the rolling wheels of buggies masked the sound of their lovemaking.

"Our Father, who art in heaven —" Doll croaked as Mingo pounded into her.

"Stop that!" he warned.

"Hallowed be Thine name . . ."

Mingo closed his hand over her mouth.

After he was done with her — wait, I think the correct thing to say here is: After *she* was done with *him* — Mingo patted Doll on her ass and said, "Fix yourself up, you look a mess."

She hadn't taken offense when Mingo pressed his filthy hand over her mouth, but for some reason the pat to her bottom struck her as impolite and disrespectful.

"How dare you," she hissed, and then struck him hard across his face. "Don't you know that I am the wife of a reverend?"

The assault took Mingo by surprise. His

hand curled into a ball. "W-woman," he stammered between clenched teeth as he patted the damp soil in search of his cigarette. When he found it, he slipped it between his lips and began to laugh at the absurdity of the situation.

"What's so funny?" Doll asked.

He didn't answer her question, he just kept laughing, even as he tugged his trousers up around his waist.

August was sitting in the living room when Doll walked into the house covered in mud. At the sight of her, he sat straight up and his face went bright with alarm.

"Doll, what happened to you?" he asked as he stood and moved toward her.

Doll looked stupidly down at her soiled clothing. "I think I fell down the river bank."

August frowned. "You think?"

"I did," Doll mumbled. "I slipped down the river bank."

"My goodness!" August declared as he took Doll gently by the elbow and guided her up the stairs. "Are you hurt?"

"I don't think so."

"Why were you walking so close to the edge?"

Doll tried her best to remember, but couldn't. "I lost the oranges," she whispered. "The bag broke and they tumbled

122

into river and I went after them."

"You went after them? Oranges? You went after some stupid ole oranges?"

Doll nodded ashamedly.

August snaked his arm protectively around her waist. "Thank God it was the oranges that rolled into the river and not you."

CHAPTER FIFTEEN

By April of 1927, most folk in Mississippi couldn't think of anything but rain, mud, mosquitoes, and flooding.

Not a drop of rain had fallen between May and July of 1926, but on the first day of August the skies opened up and remained that way for a very long time.

Bullet rain. Bucket rain. Rain as soft as rose petals. Mist.

You'd think that so much water would have washed the stench of sin right out of the air, but it didn't. The water infused it, transforming it into an invisible vapor that hung in the air like fog.

Sin was what was on August's mind when he shrugged on his gray slicker and shoved his Bible into one of the oversized pockets. Retrieving an umbrella from the stand in the small vestibule, he opened the door and stepped out into the downpour.

It was Good Friday and he was headed to

the church a few hours early to go over his sermon. It gave him no pleasure to be thinking about sin on one of the most blessed days of the Christian calendar, but try as he might, he could not shake the troubling thoughts, nor could he decide if the sin had ushered in the rain or the rain had made way for the sin. Whatever the case, both the sin and the rain were there — growing mightier with each gray, wet day.

Weeks earlier, one parishioner after the next had approached him with: "Reverend, could I have a word, please?"

August listened quietly and intently as the men confessed to gambling, drinking, and fornicating. The women's offenses were light in nature compared to their male counterparts. Their transgressions involved gossiping and coveting. August prescribed scripture and prayer and sent them on their way.

But he soon realized that sin hadn't infected just his community; it was wreaking havoc all across the state. Every new day brought another horrendous report of evildoing:

William N. Coffey, aged 48, confessed he'd murdered his bigamous bride, Hattie Hale Coffey, clubbing her to death with a baseball bat and then tossing her into the

Mississippi River.

In the town of Alligator, plantation owner V.H. McCraney shot and killed plantation owner C.G. Callicott and then put the pistol to his head and blew his brains all over the face of the wide-eyed witness, Richard Moore.

MISSISSIPPI LEADS IN NEGRO LYNCH-
INGS . . .

Yes, sin was everywhere. It had even breached the sanctity of his own home.

At the church, August removed the skeleton key from his pocket, shoved it into the lock, and turned. Once inside, he loaded the pot-bellied stove with wood and paper and tossed in a lit match. As he stood watching the flames swell and flicker, his mind wandered to his wife and the bite mark on her thigh.

He'd noticed it weeks earlier as she lay sleeping. Sometime during the night, her restless tossing and turning had caused her gown to roll up and around her waist. The warm and humid day had ushered in an equally uncomfortable evening, so the blanket was left folded at the foot of the bed and husband and wife slept uncovered.

The morning August realized that sin had taken up residence in his home was a morning similar to the thousand others that preceded it. August had risen early, swung his legs over the side of the bed, stretched his arms high above his head, and yawned.

As always, he took a moment to admire his beautiful sleeping wife, and that's when he spotted the bite, which he first took as a bruise.

On closer inspection, August could plainly see the teeth marks in her flesh, and his heart dropped out of his chest. Some man, some heathen, had placed his mouth so close to —

August stopped the thought barreling down on him.

How could she? Why would she?

Doll had not allowed him to make love to her in *that way* for months. She had even prohibited the normal coupling that occurred between man and wife. After a while, August had been forced to pleasure himself in the solitary darkness of the outhouse.

Now it was all clear to him: she had taken a lover.

Adulteress!

The word alone was kindle for fury.

No one would have faulted August if he

had snatched Doll up by the throat and choked the breath out of her.

But not August. He did what he always did when it came to Doll's misgivings — he turned her sin onto himself and absorbed like a sponge. He convinced himself that he had allowed his church and his flock to take precedence over his wife. The result of which were feelings of neglect within Doll. She in turn had sought attention elsewhere, and had stumbled into the arms of a heathen who plied her with sweet lies all in the name of pilfering her pyramid.

He had only himself to blame.

August exited the bedroom on legs made of jelly. He thought he might vomit and rushed to the outhouse. Standing in the darkness, he waited patiently for the surge, but it did not come. What did emerge were tears accompanied by a howl so loud and sorrowful that it woke Hemmingway from her slumber.

The door of the church opened and closed. August turned around to find one of his parishioners stepping in.

"Morning, Sister Betty."

"Morning, Reverend." Sister Betty's response was cheerful. "Happy Good Friday to you!"

August smiled. "And the same to you."

Sister Betty removed her coat and gave it two good shakes, sending droplets of water through the air. "I know you ain't s'pose to question God, but I gotta ask why in the world he sending down all this rain!" She chuckled as she moved to August's side and floated her hands over the stove. "Ooh, nice and toasty," she moaned.

August excused himself. He went to the small windowless room located at the back of the church. Once inside, he lit a candle, sat down at his desk, opened the drawer, and removed six pages of notes.

He'd been working on the sermon for nearly two weeks, but now, as he scanned the paragraphs, none of it read familiar. It was as if some other man had written the words. A man consumed with grief and riddled with self-pity.

You ask, *Did he question Doll about the love-bite?* No. Not one word was uttered. August buried it, alongside his pride.

Hurt is a growing thing. August's hurt took root and sprouted vines that coiled around his heart and stomach. Chest pains and a severely decreased appetite left him shaky and thin.

Hemmingway had asked, "Daddy, you feeling okay?"

August had nodded, forced a smile, and nodded again.

Doll didn't seem to notice that her husband was disintegrating right before her very eyes. If she did, well, Esther didn't allow her to give a good goddamn. And by this point in the story you should be well aware that Esther's devotion to anyone other than herself was as shallow as a saucer.

August read and reread the paragraphs; drew thick lines through sentences and scribbled notes in the margins, all the while aware of the sound of the rain beating down on the roof as loud and resolute as an army of men marching off to war.

On Candle Street, Cole was preparing to send his wife off to attend the wedding of a family member in New Orleans. Melinda was upset that Cole could not join her.

"You won't be alone," Cole reminded her. "Caress will be with you."

"But I don't know if I'm up for such a long trip."

Cole's jaw clenched in frustration. "Now, now, Lindy, you know the doctor gave you a clean bill of health."

Melinda glanced out the window. "But the rain . . ."

"It'll be nice and dry on the train." He

wrapped his arms around her shoulders. "I have to be here to receive the shipment; after that, I'm on the next train to New Orleans."

Outside, Caress was seated alongside the driver on the bench of the carriage. Her arm was going numb from holding the wide black umbrella over her head.

Cole walked Melinda to the carriage, opened the door, and helped her inside. He planted a soft kiss on her cheek.

"Don't worry, darling, I'll be there before you know it."

Cole pushed the door closed and signaled to the driver, who snapped the reins. The horses began to gallop.

It wasn't until Mingo was spotted streaking up the middle of the road with his shoulders hunched up against the downpour that people realized he hadn't been seen for days.

He was running so hard, he almost ran smack into the pair of horses that pulled the carriage carrying Melinda and Caress.

"Fool, watch where you're going!" the driver yelled.

Mingo darted toward the bridge and would have collided with Doll if she had not stepped quickly out of his path. Seeing her, Mingo came to a screeching halt. "Mrs.

Reverend, ma'am!"

Doll, whose head was tied in a yellow scarf that did nothing to protect her hair from the rain, whirled around and almost dropped the stack of records she had tucked beneath her arm. She looked at Mingo, but no recognition registered in her eyes. She offered him a polite smile and continued on her way.

Mingo watched her dodge raindrops down Candle Street before disappearing around the side of one of the houses.

He scratched his chin in bewilderment, then tugged the collar of his shirt around his neck and took shelter beneath a nearby tree. He eased himself down onto his haunches and fixed his gaze on the slate sky. He remained that way until Sam T. happened upon him.

"Hey, what you doing?"

"Huh?" Mingo blinked water from his eyes until Sam T. came into focus.

Sam T. was lean and freckled, with a mass of reddish-brown hair that he wore parted down the middle.

"You okay, Mingo?"

"Yeah. Uh-huh."

"Man, you gonna catch your death out here in the rain without a coat. Where's your coat?"

Mingo glanced down at his shirt and slacks. He seemed surprised to find that they were soaked through to the skin.

Sam T. chuckled. "You been drinking?"

"Nah."

"You sure? Why you out here in the rain?"

Mingo sniffed and slowly brought himself erect. He made a face and began stomping his feet. "I got needles all up and down my legs."

"Watch it!" Sam T. cried as he jumped away from the puddled water that Mingo splashed. He stepped under the tree and gave Mingo a long, hard look. "Ain't seen you for a few days. Where you been?"

Mingo's face went dark. "Greenville," he said with a wince.

"What were you doing in Greenville?"

"I got people there," Mingo muttered, and then brightening a bit he said, "Hey, listen, man, you got any on you?"

Sam T. understood the *any* to mean whiskey. "Nah, sorry."

"Oh," Mingo said, and the light leaked from his face.

"So, uhm, did you leave Greenville in a hurry or something?"

Mingo's eyes narrowed. "Why, what you hear?" he barked menacingly.

Sam T. raised a protective arm. "I ain't

heard nothing. It's just that it's raining and you ain't got no jacket, no slicker, no nothing on your back but that wet shirt. I just figured you left in a hurry, that's all."

Mingo smirked, and then instinctively reached for the cigarette behind his ear. When he found that it wasn't there, he patted down his shirt and dug into the pockets of his pants.

Still nothing.

Mingo gave Sam T. a hopeful look. "You got any smokes?"

Sam T. pulled out a pack of cigarettes and shook one free. It took three tries to get it lit.

Mingo took a few puffs and then pressed the tip against the bark of the tree, extinguishing it. He tucked the remainder behind his ear.

Sam T.'s eyes swung between Mingo and the road, which was beginning to look more and more like a stream.

"Me and my cousin Charlie was headed o'er to his mama's house. We weren't worrying nobody. The law just swooped down on us — guns drawn!" Mingo announced without warning.

Sam T. leaned in. "What now?"

Mingo's right eyelid began to twitch. "The law come up behind us and stuck their guns in our backs. One man say, *Can't you see its raining, boys?* Well, of course we could see that, wasn't no getting around seeing it. We weren't really understanding what point the man was trying to make. So me and Charlie said, *Yes suh, we sees that. Turn around,* the man say. And we do like he say. And then the next man raised his pistol high and brought the nozzle to rest square between my eyes, and he say: *Then why ain't you boys down by the river working?* So then I says, *Why would we be down by the river?* And that's when the first man hauled off and clobbered me upside my head with the butt of his gun."

Mingo turned his head slightly to the left and pointed to the egg-sized knot above his temple.

Sam T. examined it and grimaced.

"When he hit me, I went down, I went down hard, and sent up a might amount of mud in the process. So the one that hit me say, *First you sass me and now you dirty up my nice clean slicker? Get up, nigger!*"

Mingo's hands were shaking real hard when he snatched the butt from behind his ear and slipped it back between his quivering lips.

Sam T.'s eyes bulged. "They lock you and Charlie up?"

Mingo blew a stream of smoke from the corner of his mouth. "Nah, jail would have been a blessing. They walked us down to the river."

Sam T. frowned. "The river? For what?"

"They got most of the colored men in Greenville down at the river."

"What they got them doing down there?"

"Packing, hauling, and stacking sandbags."

Sam T. scratched his chin. "What they paying?"

Mingo shot him an incredulous look. "Paying? Nigger, ain't you heard me say the law plucked us right off the street and took us down to the river? The pay is you get to keep your goddamn life!"

Mingo sucked on the cigarette until the filter began to smoke; only then did he flick the butt out into the rain.

"Those niggers who refused to do the work were shot and thrown in the river."

Sam T. shuddered.

Mingo spat a glob of phelgm into the mud. "They emptied out the jails too."

"My God," Sam T. murmured.

"It's like a war zone up there. Men patroling both sides of the river with shotguns."

"Why is that?"

"Don't you know nothing, Sam T.?"

Sam T. shamefully shrugged his shoulders.

"If someone blow the levee closest to the north shore, the properties on the south shore might get spared. Someone blow the levee on the south shore, the property on the north shore might get spared."

"Sure nuff?"

Mingo nodded his head. "While I was there a story come down the line said that some old boys from the north shore were caught with a box of dynamite on the wrong the side of the river." He looked down at his battered shoes. "I believe they fish food now."

The two men were quiet as they watched an old woman slosh slowly up the road.

"How long they had you?"

"Two days and two nights," Mingo said in a trembling voice.

Thunder rolled across the sky and the rain began to fall in torrents. Sam T. and Mingo pressed their backs against the bark of the tree.

Mingo yelled over the din, "I finally got away —"

"Got away? They didn't just let you go?"

"I had to run."

"You run all the way from Greenville?"

"I believe so," Mingo said as he reached up and felt behind his ear. Without asking,

Sam T. offered him another cigarette.

"What happened to Charlie?"

Mingo looked off into the distance. "I don't know."

"You left him?"

"We weren't together. They drop me at one end of the river, so I assumed they took him to the other end."

Sam T. swiped rainwater from his face. When he looked at Mingo again, the man's entire body was shaking. Sam. T. gripped his shoulder.

"Gotta get you outta this weather," Sam T. urged. "I'm headed over to the church. You wanna come? Church got plenty of room and it's warm and dry inside."

"Is today Sunday?"

"Nah, it's Friday. Good Friday."

"What so good about it?" Mingo cackled bitterly.

"God, that's what's good about it," Sam T. retorted joyfully.

"Nah, Sam T., I don't think I'd be welcome."

Sam T. chuckled. "Sure you would. Everyone is welcomed in the house of the Lord."

On that rain-drenched Good Friday, Hemmingway witnessed two very interesting things as she stood staring out of her bedroom window. The first was her mother hurrying across the bridge. Doll had claimed she was going to the church to assist August with any last-minute details before service.

After Hemmingway heard the front door slam, she crossed the floor to the window, parted the curtains, and watched her mother walk in the opposite direction of the church. The fact that Doll had told a lie did not strike Hemmingway as odd, but seeing her skipping like a child through the downpour wearing a yellow scarf and carrying a stack of records was strange, even for Doll.

Normally, Hemmingway could care less about Doll's comings and goings, but she'd sensed her father's melancholy and was deeply concerned about his physical decline, which she suspected had everything to do with the love-bite on her mother's thigh.

Oh yes, Hemmingway saw it too.

The morning August's howling had startled Hemmingway out of her sleep, she lay in bed listening for a good long time. Assuming the noise was coming from a wounded animal, she closed her eyes and pulled the pillow over her face in an effort to block it out. But the pillow did little to muffle the persistent noise. Unable to take much more, Hemmingway climbed from her bed and padded down the hall to her parents' room with the intention of waking her father. She thought the two of them could seek out the animal and either attend to its wound or put it out of its misery.

The bedroom door was ajar and without knocking, Hemmingway pushed it back on its hinges. The room was filled with heather-colored, early-morning light. She saw that August was not in the bed and that Doll was still fast asleep. She walked over to the bed and was stopped short by the pink and purple bruise that seemed to glow against her mother's flesh.

Hemmingway could not mistake the mark for anything else — Paris had bitten her enough times to make her an expert.

Disgust snaked through her body.

Certainly, her father hadn't pressed his mouth so close to that place that leaked blood every month. Not the good Reverend August Hilson!

Hemmingway backed out of the room, returned to her bed, and closed her eyes. There, the longstanding repulsion she'd held for her mother turned hard with hate.

Outside, the howling finally came to an end. The outhouse door banged open and then closed and Hemmingway now understood that her father was the wounded animal.

■ ■ ■ ■

The second interesting thing Hemmingway witnessed from her bedroom window was Mingo, running so fast and so hard she thought he would take flight. The near head-on collision with the horse and then Doll slowed him down to a stop. What Mingo called out to Doll, and Doll's reply, would remain a mystery to Hemmingway. But whatever her mother had said, or *not* said, seemed to leave Mingo confused.

"You coming or what?"

Hemmingway turned around to find Paris standing in the doorway, raking a comb through his wooly hair.

"You go on ahead, I'll be there soon."

"You better not be late."

"Yeah, yeah," Hemmingway hummed, then asked, "Where's Dolly?"

Paris's face went blank.

"What do you mean? Ain't she in her room?"

Before she could respond, Paris was ambling away calling, "Dolly?" He stepped into the empty bedroom, pushed his fists into his sides, and bellowed, "Dolly!"

"She ain't here!" Hemmingway screamed from her room.

Paris reappeared with a perplexed look on his face.

"She ain't there," he said.

Hemmingway rolled her eyes. "I just said that, fool."

"Where she at?"

Hemmingway shrugged her shoulders.

Paris smirked. "Probably went to the church early," he said confidently.

"Yeah, that's probably where she went," Hemmingway replied, her voice dripping with sarcasm.

CHAPTER SIXTEEN

On Candle Street Cole Payne was in bed, propped up on four silk pillows, watching Doll dance around the room naked, save for the wet yellow scarf she wore tied around her midsection.

He'd moved the phonograph from the drawing room into the bedroom and Doll had placed the well-worn Muggsy Spanier record "I Wish I Could Shimmy Like My Sister Kate" on the turntable and was raunchily swaying her hips.

It was the first time the two had had sex in his marriage bed. Before that, they'd ravished each other in the cellar on a stack of croker sacks, and up against the walls of the shed. Once they did it in the drawing room, on the couch, while Melinda slept in the bedroom above them.

The song ended and Doll took a bow. Cole sat up and applauded. "More, more!" he cried jubilantly.

Doll happily obliged, replacing Spanier with King Oliver. She lowered the needle onto the vinyl and King Oliver began to blare: *Ev-'ry bod-y gets the blues now and then, and don't know what to do. I've had it hap-pen man-y, man-y times to me, and so have you . . .*

Doll rolled her shoulders and sang along. Cole grinned and reached for the cigar that was smoldering in the ashtray on the nightstand.

"I like that song," Cole said. "What's it called?"

Doll crossed the floor in sleek, long strides. " 'Doctor Jazz,' " she purred.

After Paris left for church, Hemmingway headed out of the house, across the bridge, and down Candle Street in search of Doll. What Hemmingway would do if she found her hadn't quite come together yet.

The street was empty, but Hemmingway could feel curious eyes watching her from behind heavy-curtained windows. Halfway down Candle, the wind snatched the umbrella out of her hands, blew it across the road and into the river. Within seconds, she was drenched.

Deflated, Hemmingway started back toward the bridge. As she passed Cole Payne's house, she thought she heard King Oliver's rippling voice exclaiming, *The more I get, the more I want, it seems* . . .

She knew that song well, because Doll played it endlessly. Hemmingway stopped and strained to hear above the roar of the rain. Soon Oliver's famous horn splintered the din and Hemmingway followed the melody straight to Cole Payne's front door.

Just as the weather turned sinister, August took his place behind the pulpit. He was so surprised to see Mingo Bailey, soaked through and shivering in the third pew, that he nodded in his direction and bellowed, "Welcome, Brother Mingo!"

Paris alone was seated in the front pew. August shot him a questioning glance, and the boy shrugged his shoulders in response.

August's mind screamed: *Probably with that man!*

Probably, August concurred with himself inwardly. *But where's Hemmingway?*

"Let us bow our heads and pray. Dear Father . . ."

Outside, the thunder clapped so loudly that the parishioners shrieked and grabbed hold of one another.

After the opening prayer, August turned to the choir. "Choir," he prompted, and the men and women burst into song.

The wind roared in protest, and August raised his arms high above his head and commanded, "Sing louder!"

Upstairs, in one of the numerous bedrooms of the Payne residence, a window banged open, shattering the glass. Cole jumped from the bed and darted from one room to the next until he came upon the mess. Rain, fueled by the wind, spewed in through the broken window and pooled on the floor.

At the church, someone looked down and saw that water was rising up through the seams of the floorboards. Another member spied it seeping in from beneath the door.

The choir continued to sing.

Outside, the wind raced around the church growling and snorting. The congregation rippled with fear.

"Stay calm, flock! Stay calm," August warned.

Downstairs at the Payne home, Hemmingway was banging furiously on the back door when the upstairs window exploded and rained down shards of glass onto her head. Panic-stricken, she snatched up a nearby flowerpot, launched it through the window of the door, snaked her hand through the ragged opening, and turned the lock.

Upstairs, Cole walked back into the room. "It's getting really nasty out there."

Doll was in the bed, stretched out on her back, admiring her fingernails. "What?"

Cole was about to repeat himself, when he heard the clatter of glass downstairs.

"What now?" he muttered as he took up one of the three oil lamps and fled from the room. With the lamplight illuminating his way, Cole bounded down the stairs.

When Hemmingway saw the beam, she hurried toward the light, hands flailing.

Cole's heart shuddered as he spotted the dark figure racing toward him. "Who's that!" he yelled, raising the lamp high into the air.

"Hemmingway Hilson!"

Cole stalled and lowered the lamp. "Who?"

From above him, Doll called out, "Oh, that's the reverend's daughter."

Both Cole and Hemmingway looked up to see Doll leaning girlishly over the banister, her bare breast swinging like church bells.

So here is the evidence, Hemmingway thought to herself as her eyes moved from

Doll to Cole and then back to Doll. "You roach!" she screamed, and took flight.

Upriver the levees gave way, and the Mississippi and all of her arteries breached their shores. The surge moved like a beast downriver, smashing through the wall of the church and toppling all but two homes on Nigger Row.

On Candle Street, Cole fought to separate mother and daughter as they clawed one another, and so none heard the growl of the approaching heave of water until it plowed through the front door. They scrambled up the stairs to safety, and stood mesmerized with horror as the water magically transformed the foyer into a pool.

Not one amongst them could swim.

"We need to go up to the attic, now!" Cole yelled.

Within seconds the lower half of the staircase was completely submerged.

Feeling scared and powerless, Hemmingway did what any child would have done in that situation: "Mommy," she said, and reached for Doll's hand.

Doll Hilson looked down at her daughter's hand and began to laugh. If Hemmingway had any bit of hope that she could ever love her mother, Doll's refusal to take her hand dashed it all away.

The house lurched; Doll swayed and shrieked with terror as she grappled to clamp hold of the very hand she'd just rejected.

Hemmingway swiftly pulled her hand from Doll's reach.

"Help me!"

The house pitched again, the staircase buckled, and Doll went reeling down into water.

Cole was stunned mute and rendered immobile. Only his eyes continued to work, swinging unbelievingly between the placid indifference on Hemmingway's face and the thrashing Doll who was struggling for her life.

"Hemmingway!" Doll gurgled as the swirling water pulled her under. "Hemm—"

Hemmingway didn't move. Cole couldn't move.

Doll's head disappeared beneath the water, resurfaced, and then disappeared again. Soon after, Esther's spirit floated up toward the ceiling and perched on the chandelier.

The next day, the sky spread itself across Mississippi in a serene blanket of baby blue.

And after months of obscurity, the sun returned, white bright and hot.

CHAPTER SEVENTEEN

The Manning brothers were blue-eyed, blond-haired young men who enjoyed fishing. They spent most Saturdays out in their rowboat drinking beer, smoking cigarettes, and reeling in bass.

When the rains stopped, they used their boat to rescue the living and the floating dead. They were the ones who found Cole and Doll.

Inside the Payne house on Candle Street, furniture, dishes, and silver picture frames holding sepia-colored photos bobbed lazily in the dark water. Overhead, the chandelier swayed, as if guided by an invisible hand.

Vance, the larger of the twins, sat at the helm of the boat slowly ranging his eyes over the water. His twin, Preston, rowed the oars.

"Hello! Hello, anybody here!" They called over and over in their baritone voices.

"Up here!" Cole shouted back.

Preston guided the boat to the staircase

and Vance climbed out. The swell of water hit his six-foot frame at the chest. He grabbed hold of the banister and pulled himself up onto the remaining steps. On the landing, he sloshed down the corridor and entered the first room he came upon.

"Hello?"

"Up here! In the attic!"

Vance turned around and started back the way he'd come. Spotting a closed door catty-corner to the room he had just walked out of, Vance grabbed the doorknob and turned. He was startled to see a wide-eyed, shivering Cole standing at the top of the short staircase.

"Hey, good to see ya," Vance said.

"And you!"

Cole extended a trembling hand. Vance took it and the two men shook.

"You alone?"

Cole shook his head. "Me and a young girl."

Hemmingway peeked out from behind Cole's back.

Vance considered her before declaring, "Well, we got enough room for both of you."

In the boat, Cole surveyed his surroundings in quiet horror. Hemmingway folded her knees to her chest and nervously chewed on her bottom lip.

"I see something," Vance said, pointing toward the drawing room. Cole strained to see and was sorry that he did. There was Doll, floating on her back, eyes wide and staring, breasts bobbing in the water like buoys.

"Don't look," Cole whispered to Hemmingway.

"We'll have to come back for the body later," Preston said as he navigated the boat through the opening where a beautiful oak door had once hung.

As they floated out of the house, Esther swooped down from the chandelier and settled on Hemmingway's shoulder.

Outside, it seemed to Cole that all of the waters of the world had converged in Mississippi.

They headed upriver to Greenwood, where there was dry land. On their journey, the group passed dozens of somber-faced men piloting rowboats crammed with people wearing stricken expressions. Some boats hauled dead bodies stacked one atop the other like sacks of potatoes. One boat carried a pair of bleating goats and a grim-faced old woman.

Every so often, someone would cry out, "Over here!" and the boats would make their way across the water and encircle the corpse like sharks.

Along the way, Vance reached into the bib of his overalls and pulled out a bag of tobacco and rolling paper. He shoved it in Cole's direction.

"No, thanks," Cole murmured.

Whistling a chipper tune, Vance sifted the tobacco onto the paper, rolled it into a line, and slipped it into the corner of his mouth.

With her eyes closed against the sun and the horror, Hemmingway allowed her body to lean and rock in tempo with the sway of the boat.

"Hemmingway?" Cole called.

"Yes?" she responded without opening her eyes.

"You okay?"

When her eyelids slowly parted, the steely gaze she fixed on Cole spoke volumes: *My mama's dead, the rest of my family probably dead too. The town is underwater. I'm hungry and I'm scared. So what do you think?* Hemmingway silently watched him until Cole felt his cheeks blaze.

"You see that?" Vance pointed at a balloon of white material.

Preston leaned over the side of the boat and squinted. "Yeah, I see it," he answered,

and began to pull the oars with great feroc-
ity.

The nose of the boat rammed into the
body with a loud thump. The collision tilted
the craft dangerously to one side and both
Hemmingway and Cole yelped in terror.

They'd rammed into a young boy dressed
in slacks and a white shirt knotted at the
neck with a bow tie.

"Oh God," Cole whispered.

Preston sucked air, and shook his head in
dismay. "That's Eula's boy."

"Oh yeah?" Vance looked closer. "Which
one?"

"J.W."

Preston set the oars, reached down between his legs, and retrieved a large hook
normally used to move bales of cotton. He
leaned over, slipped the hook beneath the
waistband of the boy's trousers, and tugged.

The body slammed into the side of the
boat.

"Lemme help," Vance said, and caught
hold of the boy's shoulders. Together, the
brothers hauled the lifeless body into the
boat.

Short dark hair fanned out across J.W.'s
scalp in slick, wet points. His eyes were open
and vacant. The mouth hung ajar, and was
filled with swarming bottle flies.

"Yeah, that's J.W. for sure," Preston said as he slapped water from his hands.

Vance combed his fingers through his hair and moaned, "This is going to kill Eula."

Preston nodded in agreement.

Vance removed his shirt, and just before he placed it over J.W.'s face, Esther executed a perfect swan dive off of Hemmingway's shoulder and plunged right into that boy's open mouth.

In Greenwood, the riverbank looked like a battlefield. Scores of people walked aimlessly about hauling items they had rescued from the waters. Many huddled under trees and beneath makeshift tents. The infirm lay stretched out on the wet grass, with friends or family members stationed at their hips.

When the Manning brothers hauled their boat up onto the muddy bank, Hemmingway leapt out, staggered to a nearby tree, and puked.

Cole, weak and nauseous himself, offered to help the brothers carry the dead boy, but Vance waved him off, plucked J.W.'s body from the boat, and slung him over his shoulder as if he was as light as a twig.

"There's a house up the hill there," Preston announced. "The people will give you water and food." His eyes moved to Hem-

156

mingway and lingered. "Uhm," he moaned, pointing his chin downriver, "she gotta head that way, to the colored camp."

Cole nodded as he watched Vance make his way over a small mound of mud and rubbish.

"Where is he taking him?" Cole asked.

"Funeral home," Preston responded.

Six months earlier, Charles Williams and Thomas Lord had opened the doors to their brand-new funeral parlor. Since then, they'd only managed to snag three percent of the business in and around Greenwood. That equaled thirty-two corpses. Thirty-two and a half if you counted the stillborn baby. The remaining ninety-seven percent went to the forty-year-old community staple: Ross and Sons.

Business was so bad that Williams and Lord had decided to throw in the towel, and just two days before the flood they had officially closed their doors.

But the havoc God wreaked on Mississippi had resulted in good fortune for Williams and Lord. Business, of course, was now booming. They couldn't believe their good luck, and when out of sight of the bereaved, it was all they could do to keep from grinning.

Vance delivered J.W. Milam's body to the funeral home and then went off to locate the dead boy's mother.

J.W.'s body was taken to the brightly lit preparation room. Williams and Lord owned only two silver gurneys and those were already occupied — so they undressed J.W.'s body and propped one chair beneath his head and another beneath his feet. A large block of ice was positioned below his body to keep it cool and a penny was placed on each eyelid.

CHAPTER EIGHTEEN

Eula Milam was a short, rotund woman with large dark eyes. She wore her wavy black hair pinned in a loose bun atop her head. She arrived at the Williams and Lord funeral home flanked by her son Fleming and Vance Manning. Mr. Lord led them into a large room with walls covered in bright white tile in the shape of playing cards. The room was filled with more than a dozen bodies and at the sight of so much death, Eula's legs turned to rubber.

"He's just over here," Mr. Lord said.

Vance and Fleming hooked their hands under Eula's arms and guided her toward her son.

"He look like he's asleep," Eula whispered. She wrung her hands and wailed, "Oh, my boy. My sweet, sweet boy!"

In a moment of dramatic grief, Eula Milam threw herself onto J.W.; the weight of her body caused the chairs to shoot out from beneath J.W. and both mother and dead son crashed down onto the melting block of ice. The pennies went skidding across the floor and fell into the drain.

Fleming ran screaming from the room, while Vance and Mr. Lord stood watching in stunned silence as Eula flopped around like a fish on land.

Eula grabbed hold of J.W.'s hand and cried, "Oh, God, why, why!"

The men took her meaty arms and tried to pull her upright, but she remained sprawled on the floor, clinging for life to her son.

"Please, Mrs. Milam, please," Mr. Lord begged.

"Goddammit, Eula, turn that boy loose!" Vance ordered.

"Ouch, Mama, lemme go!"

Mr. Lord stared at Vance and Vance returned the man's perplexed gaze. They both peered down at Eula, whose eyes were fixed on J.W.'s heaving chest.

Now, you may doubt that this actually happened. But I have no reason to lie to you. People coming back from the dead is a phenomenon that can be traced all the way back to the Old Testament of the Bible. Just the other day I became aware of a sixty-year-old woman who was hospitalized for an unexplained illness. In the night, her heart stopped beating and the physician pronounced her dead. She was taken to the morgue and her children were called. When the children arrived to identify the body, the old woman's eyes popped open and she began to cough.

Across the world in Nigeria, a Muslim woman died in childbirth and within twenty-four hours, her still body was bathed, wrapped in white muslin cloth, turned onto its side, and placed in the ground. As the mourners recited the Quranic verse and poured handfuls of soil into the grave, the woman flipped over, sat up, and began clawing at the shroud she had been encased in.

Medical officials blame the occurrence on human error. They even have a term for it: Lazarus syndrome. The religious, of course, give the glory to God. However, the culprit in the resurrection of J.W. Milam was none other than Esther.

Days later the waters started to recede, and the dead began to thoroughly reveal themselves.

Floating bodies. Bodies in trees, trapped in houses. Bodies attached to hands thrust like flagpoles from mountains of mud.

Even the undertaker, who had made a career of dealing with the dead and their survivors, became overwhelmed with grief and broke down in tears.

For the ones who could be coffined, there were funerals. August, Doll, and Paris were laid to rest alongside one another.

The missing and unaccounted for were memorialized. Melinda Payne and her faithful servant Caress fell under that category.

For years Cole would grieve and torture himself for three things he had no control over: his love-struck heart, the flood, and Doll's death.

Hemmingway had her cross to bear as well. She had watched Doll die. Had in fact had a hand in her death. At the funeral she looked calmly into her mother's dead, bloated face, and afterward she stood watching as the gravediggers covered the coffin with dirt. Even so, she was not confident that Doll was *really* dead, and she would live the rest of her days glancing over her shoulder expecting to see Doll: teeth bared, clutching a butcher knife, charging toward her. Or worse yet — Doll smiling, face lit up with her arms fanned out in anticipation of a hug.

■ ■ ■ ■

It took three months of repair before the house on Candle Street was made livable again. Workers attacked the water-damaged walls with hammers, picks, and chisels, chopping away plaster and wooden laths until they reached the joists and studs. Those they dissembled, removed, and replaced with new ones. Rock laths were nailed onto the studs and three layers of gypsum plaster were smoothed on and left to dry.

The oak floors, staircase, and the veranda were all removed and replaced. New furniture, icebox, and stove were purchased and installed.

By Independence Day, that house on Candle Street looked brand new beneath the burst of the brilliant red, white, and blue fireworks.

Hemmingway became his new maid, not for any reason other than the simple fact that she was an orphan and he, a widower — so all they had were each other.

For a while she lived in the room that Caress had once occupied. Well, Caress still owned that space, and occasionally made her presence known by throwing her ghostly weight against the walls and rattling the frosted light fixtures.

It didn't bother Hemmingway in the least. She had spent the first half of her life battling the dark spirit that was her mother, and so if Caress were trying to unnerve her, she would have to step up her efforts.

Sometimes she would go to the bridge and stare across at what once was. Birds and squirrels had taken up residence in the two remaining homes on Nigger Row. In three more years, March winds would level the houses and tall grass would grow up and around the rubble.

Widower and orphan led a quiet life. Hemmingway kept the house spotless, his clothes clean, and his belly full.

One Sunday she recreated Doll's johnny-cakes. When she placed the plate before him, Cole began to weep and the rain of tears drenched the cakes, turning them back into lumps of sweet, sticky dough.

CHAPTER NINETEEN

When Charlotte Custer knocked on the front door in the fall of 1929, Hemmingway despised her immediately.

"Afternoon, ma'am."

It was the parasol Charlotte held over her head. Hemmingway hated parasols and so instantly hated any woman who carried one.

"Is Mr. Payne at home?"

A hazel-eyed, blond-haired, prissy little snake. She wore a bonnet and laced gloves that climbed all the way to her elbows.

"No, ma'am. Who may I say was calling?" Hemmingway asked the question and broke the cardinal rule of the South when she brazenly looked directly into the white woman's eyes.

"You may say that Charlotte Custer came to call on him."

Charlotte Custer? What ole type of stupid name was that? Hemmingway wondered as she raised her hand to her mouth and coughed a laugh into her palm.

"When do you expect him to return?"

Hemmingway could feel the smirk still resting on her lips, so she kept her hand positioned over her mouth. "Thursday, ma'am."

Charlotte Custer frowned. "Oh dear," she murmured before extracting an embroidered kerchief from her sleeve and using it to swab her forehead. "That's three days away, isn't it?"

"Yes, ma'am."

"Oh dear," she moaned again. "Well, that is that then. I will return in three days."

Hemmingway watched her walk down the steps to the waiting carriage.

In three days Charlotte Custer returned, without the parasol. This did nothing to endear her to Hemmingway.

Hemmingway showed Charlotte into the drawing room, invited her to sit, and then went to fetch Cole.

"I don't trust her," Hemmingway hissed from the doorway.

Cole was working on his bottle art. But unlike other enthusiasts of the craft, he did not construct miniature boats in his bottles — he constructed Native American teepees.

"Indian houses?" Hemmingway had questioned the first time Cole showed her his work.

"Well, yes and no," Cole responded. "They're called teepees."

A year after the flood, Cole had begun to talk about taking a trip out west.

"For what?" Hemmingway had asked.

"Just to see."

"What's to see?"

"Well, the Pacific Ocean for one."

"Ain't you had your fill of water?"

The only time Cole had ever stepped foot outside of Mississippi was to visit Melinda's cousins in the neighboring state of Louisiana, and he hadn't even wanted to make that trip. But since the flood — since he had cheated death and survived to tell the tale — Cole had started to wonder about the world beyond Mississippi. When his wondering transformed into yearning, he went out and purchased a black 1928 Ford Model A and announced to Hemmingway that he was going to drive it all the way to the California coast.

Hemmingway had simply shrugged her shoulders and said, "Okay, have fun."

Cole was gone for two and a half months. When he returned, he was freckled, brown as lightly toasted bread, and filled with stories of Indians.

Hemmingway had listened, and yawned as Cole droned on and on about their customs, traditions, and the brutality they'd suffered under the white man's occupancy.

"Yeah, well," Hemmingway reminded him on various occasions, "black folk still suffering."

Cole dedicated one of the empty rooms to his craft. Bottles of all sizes and shapes lined the baseboard like glass soldiers. Boxes containing sheets of canvas, oil paints, brushes, needles, and odd-shaped tools were strewn haphazardly around the room.

He now owned volumes of books on the American Indian. Books paged through so often, the spines had split and the pages were creased and wrinkled.

Cole's most prized Indian collectible was a framed sepia-colored photograph of Geronimo. He had paid a pretty penny for the original print, which was taken in 1913 by the renowned photographer Adolph Muhr. Cole referred to Geronimo as "the greatest Indian chief ever known."

Hemmingway didn't think the man looked great at all, he just looked like an old man dressed in a shabby suit.

Cole looked up from his tedious task, pushed his wire-rimmed frames up onto his forehead, and said, "You don't trust who?"

Hemmingway sighed and stepped into the room. "That woman downstairs, the one I told you about."

Cole smirked. "What's her name again?"

"Charlotte Custer."

"Did she say what she wants?"

Hemmingway shook her head.

"Oh, okay then." He rose from the chair, unzipped his pants, and shoved his shirttails inside his waistband. "Bring us some lemonade," he said as he brushed past her. "But no cookies, I don't want her to feel like she can dawdle."

Upon entering the parlor, Cole extended his hand and said, "Miss Custer?"

Charlotte nodded.

"Cole Payne. Sorry to keep you waiting. How can I help you?" He took a seat across from her.

"Mr. Payne," Charlotte began in a syrupy-sweet voice, "it is so nice to finally meet you."

Her words melted into babble in Cole's ears. His mind was upstairs, hovering over his latest masterpiece. So reluctant was he to be there in that room with that woman, whose name had already faded from his mind, that he didn't even notice how incredibly beautiful she was.

To say he had sworn off women would not be a fair statement. But a man does not easily recover from the loss of a wife and a lover all in one day. His heart was still healing, the scab tender enough to remind him that love, and the loss of it, was painful.

Hemmingway entered the room carrying a pitcher of lemonade and two glasses.

"Oh, thank you so much," Charlotte said.

Hemmingway shot Cole a piercing look before exiting the room.

Charlotte reached for her glass, raised it to her lips, and took two small sips. She made a face, then set the glass down.

"Something wrong, Ms. Custer?"

"It's just a little tart for my taste."

"Tart?"

No one could accuse Hemmingway of making tart lemonade. If an allegation could be leveled, it would be that she made it too sweet. Cole raised his glass to his mouth, took a large gulp, and gagged.

Tart was kind — the mixture was downright sour!

"Sorry," Cole murmured, and glanced at the doorway. "I can have her make another batch if you like."

Charlotte shook her hand. "No, don't worry. I can't stay." She stood up. "I just wanted to meet the man who had so much interest in my family. Now I have met him."

The smile she offered was as big and bright as the sun, it lit up her face in a way Cole could not ignore.

"Your f-family?" he stammered stupidly. "I'm confused, Miss . . . uhm . . ."

Charlotte continued to smile. "I knew you weren't listening." She wagged a delicate finger at him. "I could see it in your eyes."

Cole gave her a sheepish look.

"Well," Charlotte sighed, and eased back down into the chair, "a friend of a friend passed one of your letters onto me . . ."

"Letters?"

"Yes." Charlotte opened the clam-shaped purse that dangled from her wrist, pulled out an envelope, and handed it to him.

Cole studied the script; it was his.

Mr. T. Farmer
Sherman Publishing House
89 Park Avenue
New York City, NY

The letter was dated December 1928. He quickly scanned the paragraphs before looking back up at Charlotte. "I don't understand."

The woman, still smiling, shifted a bit in her seat. "Is that not a letter written by your

171

own hand, Mr. Payne?"

"Yes."

"In the letter you refer to Mr. Farmer's book, *Forever, Monahseetah,* do you not?"

"I do."

"You wanted to know if Mr. Farmer had located the children of Monahseetah and General Custer. Is that correct?'

Cole nodded.

"I am the granddaughter."

Cole blinked. "The granddaughter of whom?"

Charlotte's smile turned bland. Even Hemmingway, who was eavesdropping in the hall, bristled with frustration.

"Of General Custer and Monahseetah," Charlotte replied pointedly.

It took another moment for Cole to comprehend what the woman sitting across from him had just said.

"You?"

Charlotte bobbed her head.

His obsession with Native American culture had led him to the book entitled *Forever, Monahseetah,* written by Theodore Farmer, which chronicled the love affair between Monahseetah and the famed Civil War and Indian War hero, General George Armstrong Custer.

In the book, the author claimed to have

located and interviewed the aged Monahseetah on a Cheyenne reservation in Oklahoma. Farmer wrote that Monahseetah had
been quite candid with him about her
relationship with the general and the children she had borne him — a boy in January
of 1869, and in December of that same
year, a girl.

The boy, called Yellow Bird, had Monahseetah's brown complexion and dark eyes,
but not her ink-colored hair. His locks were
light brown streaked with blond. Unfortunately, he did not live to adulthood.

Of the girl, Farmer wrote, *"The one whose
existence had been disputed for decades was
born on the thirteenth of December in 1869.
She was named Namid, which means Star
Dancer in the Cheyenne language. Namid
favored her father, as she had inherited his
blond hair and fair skin."*

As Namid grew older, her appearance
became the source of ridicule from the other
children in the community. They called her
ghost-face and pale-face and refused to play
with her.

It broke Monahseetah's heart to have her
daughter be ostracized by her own people.
So, when Namid turned eight, Monahseetah took her off the reservation and left her

with an order of nuns who ran an orphanage.

"She was such a beautiful white child, I knew someone would adopt her," Monahseetah told Farmer.

When Farmer asked, "Did you ever see her again?" Monahseetah's eyes welled with tears and her lips trembled. "Yes, every night in my dreams I see her and she is still just eight years old and very lovely to look at."

Cole had written the letter to Farmer hoping that he could reveal the exact location of the reservation, as he wanted to visit it himself and perhaps speak to Monahseetah. But Farmer never responded and Cole had not sent a second inquiry. Now here was this woman, claiming to be the granddaughter.

"So you are the child of Namid?"

Again, Charlotte bobbed her head. "My mother was adopted and raised by a family in Louisiana. When she was sixteen, she married a man named Jean Batiste. He is my father." She paused. "*Was* my father. He died from cancer to his brain in 1926. My mother followed him to heaven last year."

"Batiste? But you said your surname is Custer."

Charlotte folded her delicate hands in her lap. "Yes, I had it legally changed to Custer."

"Why?"

"To honor the memory of my grandfather."

"Your father must not have been very happy with that."

"I did so after his death." Her eyes turned sad. "Although, I will admit that he and I did not have the best relationship."

Cole leaned forward. "And your grandmother, Monahseetah?"

"Dead as well."

Cole leaned back. His face shadowed with disappointment. He raised his right hand and wrapped his fingers around his chin. "But how did you get the letter?"

"My mother told me everything about her life before she was sent to the orphanage. When the book was published, she bought a copy and we read it together. I sent a letter of introduction to the author, and a week later he came to Oklahoma to visit me and my mother. He was a very kind man."

Charlotte reached down and ran her finger along the rim of the glass.

"He said he wanted to write a story about my mother and me. We of course agreed. He went back to New York and we never heard from him again. I learned later that he had contracted pneumonia and died."

She moved her hand back into her lap.

"When the publisher received your letter, he sent it to me. It was my intention to write to you. For the life of me I don't know why I didn't." She laughed. "I've carried your letter with me for almost a year."

Cole smiled.

"Since I was here in Mississippi visiting friends, I thought I would call on you personally, to tell you how much your words meant to me." Charlotte rose again. "I've taken up too much of your time —"

"No, no. Please don't go. Would you like to stay for dinner?"

Charlotte grinned. "I would love to."

CHAPTER TWENTY

To further express her disdain for Charlotte, Hemmingway prepared a dinner of over-cooked chicken, underboiled potatoes, and freshly sliced tomatoes blanketed in salt. After dinner, they returned to the drawing room where Hemmingway served them bitter coffee.

At the end of the evening, Cole walked Charlotte to her waiting carriage. "May I call on you in Greenwood?"

"Yes, I would like that."

Hemmingway stood in the doorway glaring at them, and when Cole stepped up onto the veranda, she chirped maliciously, "Seems to me she say *yes* to everything."

"What?"

"Careful now," Hemmingway mumbled as she walked off, "I've only known whores to be that agreeable."

The next day the stock market crashed.

Hemmingway didn't quite understand what it all meant, but from the way the white people in town were running around like chickens without heads, she took it as an omen.

"You see what kind of bad luck that woman done brought on this town?"

Cole was sitting in his office with his ear hovering near the radio. The broadcast came from WJDX, located on the top floor of the Lamar Life Insurance building in Jackson, Mississippi. "Shush!" he warned.

The announcer said: *"Lines as long as the Mississippi River have formed outside of banks all around the country, as people scramble to withdraw their money."*

"Shouldn't you be in Greenwood trying to get your coins?"

"Hemmingway, please!" Cole snapped.

He wasn't very worried. He had some money in the bank, but not much. Lucky for him, last year he'd had a nightmare that ripped him from his sleep. In the dream, he'd gone to the bank to withdraw money, and was advised by the teller that all of his money had combusted. She reached down, opened a drawer, and removed a handful of ash, which she slid across the counter. "This is all that remains."

Cole was so disturbed by the dream that

he went to the bank and withdrew all but eighty-five dollars. He brought the money home, stuffed it into jars, and buried them. As for stock, he owned none.

"She evil, I tell ya!" Hemmingway roared.

Evil or not, Cole Payne was smitten, and he began courting the granddaughter of General Custer.

Within weeks, the scab covering his heart curled, withered, and dropped away. Once again, his heart drummed free and wild, and love responded like an animal in heat.

He proposed to Charlotte Custer on Christmas day.

Hemmingway was tightlipped when Cole brought her the news.

"Well, aren't you happy for me? For us?"

Hemmingway shrugged her shoulders.

"Why don't you like her?"

"Don't matter if I do or if I don't. You the one gotta lay down with her, not me."

"You watch your mouth, Hemmingway Hilson!"

They were married in February of 1930 and Charlotte Custer-Payne moved into that house on Candle Street. She placed her delicates into the dresser drawers, hung her finery in the chifforobe, and set her parasol in the umbrella stand.

You already know that from the very beginning Hemmingway didn't like Charlotte. Well, I'm sorry to tell you that the middle didn't get any better.

Hemmingway continued to sabotage their meals, and when Charlotte addressed her, Hemmingway refused to respond. Any orders that Charlotte wanted carried out had to come from Cole.

A year into the marriage, Cole was at wit's end. For the umpteenth time, he cornered Hemmingway and reprimanded her about her behavior. The young woman innocently batted her eyes and said, "I don't know what you're talking about."

The tension continued to build between the two women until it exploded in a screaming match that sent Charlotte flying from the kitchen in tears.

"She is the help! The HELP — and she talks to me like I am *her* employee!" she screamed into Cole's flustered face. "I want her gone, out, now!"

What could he tell his sweet, pretty young wife? Certainly not the truth, which was that he kept the often rude and always stubborn Hemmingway in his employ as a penance for his wrongdoings. Instead he said, "I promised her mother that I would look after her."

Charlotte was speechless and hurt. She picked up a bottle of perfume and hurled it against the bedroom wall.

Charlotte took the issue to an acquaintance, and after a long, thoughtful moment, the woman said: "White men and Negro women been a problem since forever."

Charlotte shuddered at the implication, but back on Candle Street she spat those same words in her husband's face. Cole was shocked and began to stutter his defense.

Charlotte cut him off with a sweep of her hand. "If you don't get rid of her, Cole, I swear I will smash everything in this house, and," she added with fierce conviction, "that semen sack between your legs!"

Cole, of course, acquiesced and hired a man who owned a mule and wagon to cart Hemmingway and her belongings to a small house he owned, near the center of town. Hemmingway would live there for the rest of her years.

The years inched by, and in 1936, after Cole sold off the store and the house on Candle Street and moved to another part of the state, the postman walked right up to Hemmingway's front door and placed an envelope in her hand. The contents included the deed to the house and ten crisp hundred-dollar bills.

Hemmingway hid the money away and continued to support herself by cooking and cleaning for other families on Candle Street. And like her mother, she made and sold johnnycakes. For the most part, she kept to herself.

In 1940, people began to notice that Hemmingway Hilson was putting on weight . . . in her midsection.

Not quite out of season, but no spring chicken — Hemmingway was nearly thirty years old. She didn't have a husband and no one had ever seen her keeping company with a man.

Immaculate Conception?

"Nah," someone laughed, "that only happens to white folk!"

People began placing bets on her due date — if she was in fact pregnant. She hit the waddling stage quick, so was further along than anyone had suspected.

Someone suggested that Cole Payne might be the father, even though he had moved away years earlier. That insinuation raised the stakes to include wagers on the infant's color.

"Maybe she ain't pregnant, maybe she's just fat," said the fat woman who looked pregnant.

The talk swirled and bubbled in a cauldron of gossip, but no one was bold enough to approach the often-salty woman and ask, "Hemmingway Hilson, you expecting?"

■ ■ ■ ■

PART TWO

■ ■ ■ ■

CHAPTER TWENTY-ONE

He had been such a sweet child, but after he died and came back again, he was different. J.W. was suddenly fond of torturing living things: cats, puppies, and fledglings. His own baby sister couldn't escape his cruelty — one afternoon he bound her ankles and wrists with rope, propped her up against a tree, arranged wood and dried corn husks at her feet, and set it ablaze. Thank goodness a passerby saw the smoke and heard the boy whooping like an Indian, or else the girl would have burned to cinders.

His mother, Eula, made up all types of excuses for his devious behavior: *He don't mean no harm. Boys are mischievous by nature.*

She coddled him, dubbed him extraordinary because he had died and come back to life. She called him "my little Jesus boy."

The people around town called him the devil.

When the senior Milam died, Eula married a man named Charles Bryant. He wasn't a sharecropper like her previous husband, but a businessman who owned two trucks and had purchased the grocery store from Cole Payne.

J.W. gave Charles Bryant the chills. One day he told Eula, "Something ain't right with that boy."

Eula rubbed her pregnant belly and retorted nastily, "Well, let's see what *your* seed produces."

Charles was hoping and praying for a girl, but Eula gave birth to a son, who they named Roy.

In 1942, J.W. was twenty-three years old and went down and enlisted himself in the army. He was deployed overseas where he could actively and openly pursue his burgeoning passion — murder.

He did it so well that he was awarded a Purple Heart and a Silver Star.

J.W. had departed Mississippi a scraggly specimen of a man, and returned a six-foot-two, 235-pound war hero.

"My Jesus boy!" Eula cried, and burst into tears, when he stepped out of the checkered cab.

His stepfather gave him a job as a truck

driver and J.W. bedded every willing female who lived along his delivery route, which snaked through three states.

He eventually married a thick-legged girl named Juanita and the two settled into a small house on the outskirts of this place that I am.

When they made love, J.W. set the .45 he'd brought back from Europe on the nightstand. He enjoyed having it in his sights as he rammed himself mercilessly into his wife.

Juanita knew about the gun, but not the round metal tin which once held snuff, but was now filled with teeth. Teeth from the dead Germans he'd shot and killed in the war. He'd dislodged the teeth by holding the corpse by the hair and slamming the butt of the gun into its dead mouth.

In Mississippi, J.W. tried to feed his passion by hunting deer, possum, and wild Russian boar — but killing animals didn't offer the same thrill as slaying a living, breathing human being.

When the Korean War began, J.W. went to the recruiting office and tried to enlist. By then, though, his affection for whiskey and cigars had taken its toll. The army declared him ineligible to serve and the morose J.W. went back home and drank whiskey until his eyes blurred.

Juanita had given birth to two sons at that point, and she made the sad mistake of saying, "I'm glad they ain't take you, 'cause our boys need their daddy."

J.W. flew at her, wrapped his hands around her throat, and choked her until the capillaries in her eyes exploded.

CHAPTER TWENTY-TWO

In 1955, that boy came from Chicago down here to spend the summer with his mama's people. They called him Bobo, but his given name was Emmett.

He arrived with a few casual clothes, one suit, one tie, and a white shirt that was one size too small and frayed around the collar. His black Sunday shoes were scuffed at the toe and veined with cracks. His pride and joy was a pair of brand-new navy blue Converse sneakers that his mother had saved three months to buy.

He was brown and stout with full cheeks and a generous belly that jiggled when he laughed. His ears were long and the lobes were curved upward. He wasn't anything Padagonia would look at, but Tass was head over heels.

"That boy don't even know you exist."

"Says who?"

"Says me."

"He does too, I saw him looking at me just the other day."

"What day was that? Where was I?"

"You were wherever you were and we were someplace else." Tass giggled at her wit.

Padagonia crossed her eyes and stuck her tongue out of the side of her mouth. The two laughed until Padagonia's mother stepped out onto the slanted porch and tapped the broom handle against the wooden door jamb.

"You out here playing the fool while I'm in the house working like a slave?"

Their eyes swept across Willie Tucker's gnarled toes.

"Well, what you waiting for?" Willie admonished. "Get the hominy grits out your ass!"

Padagonia sulked into the house.

"And you, Miss Ting-a-ling, I'm sure you got some chore you need to be tending to, don't you?"

Tass didn't, but she nodded her head and said, "Yes, ma'am." And scurried across the road to the house that her mother owned, free and clear.

By the time Padagonia finished her chores, the sun had taken on a tangerine color. Tass was sitting on the bottom step of her porch biting her fingernails. When she saw Padagonia emerge, she jumped to her feet and bounded across the road.

Hemmingway's face appeared behind the gray mesh screen of the door. "Girl, where you going?"

"To the store!" Tass hollered back as she and Padagonia double-timed it down the road.

The front yard of Moe Wright's home was a cemetery of rusted cars, bicycle frames, and the metal guts of farm machines. Emmett was seated on the edge of the porch, the blue jeans he wore were rolled up to his knees, and his bare feet were covered in Mississippi mud dust. He was chomping on a slice of sweet pink watermelon.

The girls stepped into the yard and Padagonia called, "Hey, Bobo," in that singsong fashion girls are partial to using.

Emmett looked up and they could see that his chin was glistening with watermelon juice. He nodded at them and winked.

Padagonia strolled into the yard and was a full five strides from Emmett before she realized that Tass wasn't at her side. "Come on, Tass," she urged with a flip of her hand.

Tass could not move. The nod was expected, but the wink he'd added unraveled her.

"Come on," Padagonia said again.

But Tass did not take a step. Instead, she bashfully dropped her chin to her chest and focused her attention on the bright red polka dots that covered her shirt.

Padagonia sighed and skipped ahead. When she reached the porch, she scaled the steps and proceeded to knock noisily on the door. "Mr. Wright! Mr. Wright!"

"He gone to town."

Emmett's voice dripped Midwestern nectar. Padagonia kept knocking, just so she could hear him say it again.

"Hey, girl, I said he ain't home, they gone to town."

"Oh," Padagonia cooed coyly before clomping across the porch and plopping down next to him.

Tass was trying hard to mask her jealousy, but even from where Padagonia sat, she could see the rush of steam streaming from Tass's nostrils.

Padagonia chuckled and beckoned Tass once again: "Come on!"

Tass turned and gave Padagonia her back.

"What's wrong with her?" Emmett asked as he tossed the rind down to the ground.

Padagonia shrugged her shoulders. "I dunno, I guess you make her nervous."

Emmett looked Padagonia full in the face.

"Yeah?"

"Yeah!" Padagonia shouted as she leapt from the porch and kicked the rind across the yard. "See you later." She darted back to Tass and whispered, "You better stop acting the fool 'fore that boy start thinking something wrong with you."

Tass sucked her teeth and started walking away. Padagonia fell into step beside her.

"Did you have to sit so close to him?"

Padagonia stopped and laughed. "What you say, Tass Hilson?"

Tass kept walking. "Did he say anything about me?"

"Yeah, he said you a few eggs short of a dozen!"

Tass turned horrified eyes on her friend. "He said that?"

Padagonia giggled. "Nah, girl, I'm just pulling your leg."

"Oh."

Padagonia stooped down and plucked a dandelion from the blanket of grass that bordered the road. "Here."

Tass offered her a lopsided grin. "Thanks." She took the weed and slipped it into her hair. "How do I look?"

"Like the cutest little country girl in Money, Mississippi."

■ ■ ■ ■

To Tass, Emmett was everywhere and present in all things. He was all over her mind, pressed into the seams between the floorboards, glowing amidst the stars, and there in the sweet swirl of sugar, milk, and butter in her morning bowl of farina.

Who knows why some fall victim to love so easily?

Tass was smitten from the very first time she laid eyes on Emmett. There was something about his smile and the way he talked; he had magnetism about him that she had never encountered before.

In the three weeks he'd been here, Emmett had barely said more than hi and bye to Tass. But it didn't matter, she had parlayed those words into reams of conversation that she played out in the privacy of her bedroom.

One afternoon, she draped her hair comb in a dingy white rag and tied a tattered black shoelace around the neck of her hairbrush. She spouted a few silly words of love and then declared, "I do!" as she brought the comb and brush together in a passionate kiss.

Hemmingway had been watching from the

doorway. When she stepped into Tass's bedroom her eyes were sparkling with amusement.

"What in the world are you doing?"

"Nothing," Tass offered ashamedly.

"Child, you silly enough for two people. Put that comb and brush back on my dresser."

Tass did as she was told and then headed outdoors where Padagonia was just crossing the road to fetch her.

"Mama gave me ten cents, said we can split it," Padagonia announced, and the best friends set out for Bryant's grocery store.

Outside the store, at the center of a circle of fawning girls, was Evelyn Hall. Evelyn's mother lived in New York City and sent her crinoline skirts and patent-leather shoes which her grandparents allowed her to wear any day of the week she chose.

When Evelyn looked over and saw Padagonia and Tass approaching, she flicked her shiny Shirley Temple curls and waved.

"Hey, Padagonia! Hey, Tass!"

The circle parted and Tass and Padagonia stepped in.

"What you got?" Padagonia asked, pointing to the heavy brown paper bag Evelyn clutched in her hand.

"Gum balls, lemon drops, lollipops, Mallo

Cups, and licorice."

Padagonia and Tass exchanged glances.

"All of that?" Tass breathed in awe.

"Yeah, my mama sent me a whole dollar."

Padagonia's eyes popped. "A whole dollar?"

"Yep, she got a new daddy for me. A new rich daddy," Evelyn said as she playfully twirled a greasy curl around her index finger.

As far as Tass had heard, this was the *third* new daddy Evelyn's mother had acquired that year.

"Oh, well, that's nice," Padagonia said, and tugged her friend toward the store. "Come on, Tass."

Evelyn held up her bag of sweets. "Y'all could have some of mine if you want."

"Really?" Tass beamed and reached for the bag.

Padagonia slapped her hand away. "Thanks, but we have money."

Tass glared at her. "But she offered —"

"We don't need her charity," Padagonia retorted between clenched teeth.

"Suit yourself then," Evelyn said with a smirk.

The circle around Evelyn closed and the poorest of the poor greedily held out their hands for a piece of her sweet charity.

Inside the store the ceiling fans whirled noisily. Tass and Padagonia floated from one candy-filled fish bowl–shaped jar to the next.

Carolyn Bryant, the wife of the store-owner, closed the comic book she was reading and asked, "Y'all know what you want?"

"Lemon drops," Tass piped.

"Wait a minute now," Padagonia said as her eyes continued to skip over the jars. "I'm still deciding."

Tass pressed her fists defiantly into her hips and pronounced, "I'm done deciding. I don't have to wait on you. A nickel of that dime is mine." She turned to Carolyn and said, "May I have five cent worth of lemon drops, please?"

As the woman strolled over to the jar of lemon drops and unscrewed the lid, the door opened and the August heat slipped in alongside a jagged slab of sunlight. Emmett, along with a cousin and a friend, walked in.

Tass sucked air and stepped quickly behind a broad wooden beam.

The boys acknowledged Padagonia and raised a friendly hand to Carolyn, who responded with a "Hey, boys."

They went to the cooler and retrieved three bottles of Coca-Cola, and then each of them placed a nickel on the counter and started toward the door.

A jar of pickles caught Emmett's eye and he doubled back to the counter to take a closer look. After a moment of close examination, he swiped his hand across his forehead and let off a long, shrill whistle. "Those are some gargantuan pickles!"

Tass had never heard the word *gargantuan.* Unable to contain herself, she popped out from her hiding place and asked, "What that mean?"

Emmett turned around and grinned. "That means really big." His gaze floated back to the jar. "I believe I would like to have me one of them gargantuan pickles!"

"I ain't never in my life heard someone whistle like that," Carolyn snickered as she unscrewed the top from the jar and stuck her hand inside.

Emmett made a face. "Ain't you got nothing to fish it out with?"

Carolyn kept reaching. "Nope, just my fingers." She pinched a pickle between her thumb and forefinger. "Got it!"

Emmett rocked back on his heels and whistled again. "That sure nuff is a big sucka though!"

Carolyn giggled and nodded her head in agreement. "Where you learn to whistle like that?" she asked as she wrapped the pickle in wax paper and handed it to him.

"Back home. Chicago," Emmett proudly replied as he reached for the pickle. "How much?"

"Two cents."

Carolyn couldn't help but notice the large ring on Emmett's finger. "Is that real silver?"

Puffing his chest out like a blowfish, Emmett declared, "Yes, ma'am, it is."

Carolyn leaned in and squinted at the letters:

May 25
1943
LT

"You LT?"

"LT stands for Louis Till. That's my daddy." His words carried the slightest hint of sadness. "*Was* my daddy. He was killed in the war."

"Oh," Carolyn said without offering any condolences.

When Emmett stepped out of the store, his cousin yelled, " 'Bout time!"

Tass and Padagonia followed and Emmett

asked if they were headed back home. The girls nodded.

"Well, we might as well all walk together then," he said.

Evening was inching in and it brought with it a breeze that set the tree limbs to quivering and raised goose bumps on Tass's bare arms.

The group walked along in silence. Tass didn't need any words, she was happy enough being in such close proximity to Emmett and breathing the same air.

At the bend in the road they bid their goodbyes.

"See ya."

"Okay, bye."

The boys went left and Padagonia and Tass went right.

Padagonia glanced over at Tass and saw that her face was plastered with a wide foolish grin. She slapped her playfully on the shoulder and then sprinted away singing, "Bobo and Tass, sitting in a tree, k-i-s-s-i-n-g!"

CHAPTER TWENTY-THREE

Mid-August served up a sweltering platter of heat that demanded that people wear as little as possible in the daytime and sleep damn near naked at night.

Tass and her friends spent their days frolicking in the cool waters of the Tallahatchie River. It was there at the river's edge that Emmett finally took serious notice of Tass. She was splashing about with Padagonia and a few other girls. She didn't own a bathing suit, so she was dressed in an old blue dress. Her hat of thick hair was drenched and matted on her head like a sponge. On this day, the sight of her moved something deep within in him that he didn't know he owned.

Emmett dove beneath the surface of the water and frog-kicked his way to the circle of girls. He brushed his hands against their calves, and they jumped from the water squealing like rats.

When he reemerged he was laughing so hard, he snorted water through his nose.

"I hope you choke!" Padagonia screamed. "Damn fool!"

Emmett spat a glob of foamy saliva into the water. "Aww, come on, don't say that!"

Padagonia gave him a hard look. Tass tried to do the same, but you know she couldn't, on account of the way she felt about him.

Emmett raised his hands above his head. "Sorry. Okay? I'm sorry."

After a while, Padagonia waded back in, past the place they'd been able to stand — out toward the center of the river where she had to tread water to stay afloat. Tass inched out as well, until the water caressed her waist, and then stopped.

"You ain't coming any further?" Emmett asked.

"Can't swim," she said, and scooped up a handful of water and dribbled it down her face.

"I can teach you."

Padagonia splashed him. "And by *teach,* do you mean drown?"

A chorus of laughter rose up from the group.

"Naw, that's okay," Tass stammered as she started back toward the riverbank.

Emmett followed her out and onto the

grainy sand. He used his foot to clear away small pebbles and bits of broken tree limbs so that Tass could sit in comfort.

"Sorry I scared you," he said, and lowered himself down to next to her.

Tass could barely contain her excitement. A scream slithered up her throat and she pressed her lips together to keep it inside.

Emmett reached for a twig and used it to carve a figure of a horse in the sand. When he was done, Tass pointed at the form and said, "Horses don't have wings."

"In my dreams they do."

Tass chuckled. "Well, maybe you eating too many peaches before you go to sleep at night."

Emmett laughed and raked his hands across the image. "I can draw anything, you just tell me what."

A cat, a dog, old cock-eyed Mr. Henley — he depicted them all, perfectly.

"You draw really good."

"If you think this is good, wait till I show you what I could do with a pencil and paper."

"Who done these?"

"Emmett."

Tass preferred the tidiness of *Emmett* to the clownish, absurd nickname.

"Who?"

"Bobo, Mr. Wright's grandnephew."

"Oh," Hemmingway murmured in her throat.

Tass had tacked Emmett's drawings on her bedroom wall. Drawings on butcher paper, lined composition paper, newspaper — any type of paper he could get his hands on. At Tass's request he had drawn all sorts of magical things: winged pigs, unicorns, angels, and the buildings that made up the famous Chicago skyline.

Hemmingway folded her hands behind her back as she studied every drawing. There was one in particular that made her catch her breath. It depicted a river, and a man and woman — or a boy and girl — holding hands, their feet hovering just above the water.

Hemmingway was no Jesus freak, no Bible-beating Baptist, but something about that drawing felt sacrilegious to her and she tore it from the wall.

Tass gasped. "Mama!"

Hemmingway reeled around; her pupils were on fire. "Only Jesus walked on water," she snarled.

"It's just a picture, Mama. He didn't mean to blaspheme."

The force in her daughter's voice snapped

Hemmingway to attention and it was then that she saw the woman glowing inside of Tass.

"You certainly spend a lot of time with that boy," Hemmingway said, and then hung the bait: "You like him like *that?*"

Tass blushed and stammered, "No!"

"Let me tell you something, Tass: boys his age only have one thing on their minds!" Hemmingway aimed the tip of her index finger at Tass's groin. "You know like I know, you'll keep that purse of yours closed until you say, *I do.* And if I find out that you even thinking of doing otherwise, I'ma tear your behind up!"

And with that, Hemmingway walked calmly from the room.

When Tass heard the soup pot hit the burner, and was sure that Hemmingway was out of earshot, she whispered under her breath, "Look who's talking about purses and marriage."

Later, as the small group convened on Moe Wright's porch, Tass repeated her mother's threats for her friends.

"Aww, Tass, don't take it no kinda way," Padagonia said without moving her eyes from the checkerboard. "She just don't want you to go and get yourself in trouble like

Verna did." She then made a big show of triple-jumping Emmett's cousin Hank. "King me, nigger!" she cried triumphantly.

Hank shook his head in wonder. "How do you keep doing that?"

Emmett scratched his chin. "Verna? Who's that?"

"You don't know her. She used to live over near the Sheridan place, but her mama sent her to Philadelphia when she got in trouble."

"Trouble?"

Padagonia placed her hand just below her breast and carved an invisible arch through the air. *Trouble.*

"Oh," Emmett groaned, and then looked at Tass. "Your mama think . . . that me and you . . ."

Tass sucked her teeth. "Can we talk about something else, please?"

"King me!" Padagonia shouted again.

Hank jumped up and kicked the board off the milk crate, sending the black and white chips soaring into the air.

"Sore loser," Padagonia huffed as she scrambled to gather the chips.

Hank stomped down the steps. "I'm going to the store."

"Yeah, I guess it's time," Emmett said, and shoved his hands deep into the pockets of his trousers.

"See ya tomorrow then," Padagonia responded, and then looked at Tass. "You ready?"

Hank blinked. "Y'all ain't coming?"

"Ain't got no money," Tass said.

"Come on, I'll treat," Emmett offered.

At Bryant's grocery store, Emmett bought them all ice pops with frozen gobstoppers in the center. Hank suggested that they have a contest.

"First one to get to the gobstopper wins."

That was obvious, but the rules needed to be made supremely clear.

Licking. Only licking.

Biting was an automatic disqualification.

The first one to get to the gobstoppper would be declared the winner. The prize? The title of fastest licker in town.

They were just a few strides away from the store and already licking furiously on their ice pops when Carolyn Bryant stepped out onto the porch, pulled her chestnut hair off of her shoulders, and wrapped it into a loose knot.

Their easy laughter floated over to her and raised a smile to her lips. Maybe that's why she called out to him, because he was young and carefree and she missed that part of her life. She was still young herself, just twenty-one — but married to a man who was rarely home, and when he was home, all he wanted to do was drink beer and fuck. They never went anywhere, not even to the movies or on a picnic.

Perhaps the sight of the group of young people immersed in play and not work or marriage made her nostalgic for her own days of freedom.

In her mind she screamed, *I want to come along and play the licking game!*

But that was impossible in the world she came from and the world she lived in.

So after tying her hair into a knot, Carolyn skipped out into the road, cupped her hands around her mouth, and hollered, "Hey! Do that whistle for me again, would you?"

And he did and the sound made Carolyn happy, it made her feel included in something free and forbidden.

Unfortunately, at that very moment a green Buick was rolling up the street. It slowed as it approached the group of teenagers. When it was upon them, the driver revved the engine and spun the wheels, creating a thick cloud of dust.

The teenagers covered their ice pops with their hands and backed away from the road. A moment later, the car screeched off and disappeared down the street.

The contest continued. *Lick, lick, lick* . . .

When they reached the bend, Emmett was the clear winner. He raised the purple gobstopper victoriously into the air. "I am the king!"

Hank laughed, and gave him a shove. "The title is fastest licker in town."

"I think I should get a prize," Emmett beamed.

"Ain't nobody got nothing to give you, fool!"

"I think Tass got a prize for you, Bobo," Padagonia teased.

Tass's mouth fell open. "What?"

"Aww, man," Hank cried, and threw his hands up into the air. "Y'all been giving each other googly eyes for days now. Just go on ahead and get it over with already!"

Emmett feigned ignorance. "Get *what* over with?"

"Just kiss her! You know you want to!" Padagonia shrieked with impatience.

"W-what?" Tass uttered again.

Emmett turned to her. "You want to?"

Did she want to? Was water wet?

Tass shrugged her shoulders. "Well, if you want to," she mumbled.

"Yeah, I guess," Emmett mumbled.

"Aww, we ain't got all night!" Hank bellowed.

"Shut up, man!" Emmett said, and then grabbed Tass by the hand, gently pulled her to him, and brought his lips toward hers.

Tass would always remember the scent of the grape ice pop on his breath and the way he closed his eyes just before their lips met.

Hank yelped and clapped and Padagonia tugged Tass away, exclaiming, "Save some for another time, girl!"

Tass's head was spinning and she thought, *This is what being drunk must feel like.*

"Come on, Dorothy Dandridge."

Padagonia hooked her arm around Tass's waist. "We'll see y'all tomorrow," she yelled to the boys.

"By-eeee," Tass sang.

Emmett rolled his shoulders and waltzed toward home with the air of a young man who had a long and full life ahead of him.

Chapter Twenty-Four

"It wasn't nothing."

"Nothing? A nigger whistling at you is nothing?"

In the small apartment above the store, J.W. Milam, Carolyn's brother-in-law, paced the floor and puffed savagely on his Winston cigarette.

"Niggers are well aware that they ain't suppose to whistle at white women. They know that!"

On the couch, nursing a glass of whiskey, was Carolyn's husband, J.W.'s younger half-brother, Roy Bryant.

J.W. glared at him. "Roy!"

Roy's head popped up. "Yeah?"

"Don't you care about what the boy done to your wife?"

Roy swirled the whiskey around the glass. "Yeah, I guess so."

J.W. exploded: "You guess so? This is your wife's honor we talking about, boy!"

J.W. leapt across the room, caught Roy by the collar, hauled him off the couch, and then shoved him back down again. Roy didn't even try to defend himself. J.W. outweighed him by twenty pounds, five years, two tours in World War II, and a half a bottle of whiskey.

"Ain't you got no balls?"

Roy looked down at his hands.

J.W. snatched the whiskey bottle from the table and turned it up to his mouth.

"J.W., let's just forget about this. That boy ain't meant no harm," Carolyn insisted.

J.W. burped and slapped his chest. "I can't do it." He thumped his temple with his fingers. "I wish I could forget it, darling, but it's seared into my brain."

Carolyn wrung her hands and shot Roy a nervous look.

"Get up, boy!"

Roy shook his head. "I'm tired, J.W. Just go home and sleep it off."

J.W. eyed him for a long, intense moment, before he reached around and pulled a gun from the waistband of his trousers. He licked his fingers, smeared the saliva over the nozzle, and aimed it at Roy's heart.

Carolyn screamed and lunged at J.W. He knocked her back with one hefty swing of his arm.

"Either we gonna handle this tonight, or I'ma blow you away," J.W. sneered drunkenly.

Roy nervously licked his lips. "Okay, J.W. Whatever you say."

They barreled down the road in silence. Roy looked up at the dark sky and wondered where in the world the moon had gone off to. J.W. drained the bottle of whiskey and tossed it out the open window and then stepped down harder on the accelerator.

As they approached Moe Wright's house, the dogs in the yard barked and tugged on their chains. Inside a light came on, and soon after that Moe Wright was standing in the doorway dressed in a ragged T-shirt and striped pajama pants. He raised his hands over his eyes, squinting against the bright headlights that J.W. aimed on the house like a cannon.

"Who that?"

J.W. climbed out of the car and started toward the house. Roy followed.

"Moe, you know me, dontcha?"

Moe lowered his hand. "Yes sir, Mr. Milam, I sure do."

"Good. Look here, I come for the Chicago boy."

Moe frowned. "May I ask why, Mr.

Milam?"

J.W. turned around and looked at his half-brother. "Tell 'em why, Roy."

Roy smirked, cleared his throat, and whispered, "He, uhm — uhm, whistled at my wife."

Moe Wright's wife Mary appeared in the background dressed in a tattered pink robe. She tugged at the scarf on her head as she peered over her husband's shoulder.

"My boy? You sure 'bout that, suh?"

"Sure 'bout what?" Mary Wright whispered.

"Your nephew whistled at my brother's wife," J.W. spat. "And we come to school him on how white women are to be treated in Mississippi!"

"Mr. Milam, Mr. Bryant, you know my grandnephew ain't from 'round here, he don't know the ways of the South —"

"Well, that's why we here, Moe. We gonna teach him and we gonna teach him for free," J.W. cackled, and pushed past Moe.

Moe caught him by the shoulder. "Now wait a minute, Mr. Milam, I will whip the boy myself. I'll whip him and put him on the next train back to Chicago."

J.W. glared down at the man's black hand. "Take your hand offa me, nigga!" he sneered, and Moe's hand dropped heavy as lead down to his side.

"I don't want no trouble, Mr. Milam."

"Too late for that. Now where is he?"

Mary clutched her robe. "Moe, don't let them take him," she sobbed.

What was Moe to do? He was an old man, an old black man who only had his words, and he had used them and they had failed him.

Moe pointed down a narrow hallway.

J.W. kicked in the first door he came upon and two dark bodies sprang up from the bed. J.W. stepped in and peered at them. He couldn't make out their faces in the dark, but he knew that neither boy was the one he was looking for because they were too thin.

"Where's the nigger from Chicago?"

One lanky boy pointed at the wall.

The sound of the first door being kicked in startled Emmett and Hank, who shared a bed in the second room. They were sitting up, rubbing sleep from their eyes, when J.W. burst in.

"You!" he yelled, pulling the gun from his waistband and waving it at Emmett. "Get up and get dressed, you're coming with me."

After Emmett threw on some clothes, J.W. and Roy each grabbed one of his arms and dragged him into the front room where Moe and his wife were standing shoulder to shoulder, cradling a battered coffee can.

"P-please," Mary said as she pried the lid off the can and pulled out a roll of money. "This is all we have — one hundred and seven dollars. You can have it, just leave the boy."

J.W. and Roy stared at the roll of money, and for a moment a flicker of hope whipped in that room. But just as quickly as it came, it was gone.

"Don't want your money."

Emmett struggled to escape from their grip. His face was slick with tears. He looked at his aunt and uncle and said, "Please don't let them take me. Please!"

Mary echoed her grandnephew's request with her own shrill: "PLEASE!"

J.W. just laughed and he and Roy dragged that boy out of the house, tossed him into the backseat of the Buick, and tore off into the night.

The empty beer and Coke bottles on the car floor rolled and clashed noisily with every wild turn J.W. forced the car into.

"You gonna get yours, nigger, just wait and see. You gonna get yours real good!"

J.W. ranted and raged and pounded angrily on the dashboard, while Roy sat perfectly still with his hands folded neatly in his lap as though he might be praying.

Two miles away from the Wright home, J.W. eased his foot off the gas and the speedometer's needle dropped from 70 to 40. He turned on the radio and casually tossed his arm out of the window, his fingers drummed the car door in time with the music. They sailed along as if they were going to a baseball game or down to the river for a swim.

Roy chanced a glance at his brother's face and saw that he was smiling.

In the backseat, Emmett was shaking so bad, he thought he would shake himself right out of his skin. Try as he might, he couldn't wrap his mind around what was happening to him. He kept closing his eyes and counting back from three, hoping that when he opened them again he would be not at his uncle's house but far and away from here — back home in Chicago, in his own bed, his mother in the room next door.

He wasn't even clear as to what he had done. The words the crazy white man had shouted in his face didn't make any sense at all. A white woman? He didn't know any white women. Did he? Emmett wracked his mind but the only thing that continued to float to the surface was that he might not ever see his mother again.

J.W. pulled the car up alongside a barn and turned off the engine. "Stop your blubbering," he yelled as he reached in and yanked Emmett from the backseat. "Get the flashlight out the trunk," he ordered Roy.

The barn was empty save for a few tools hanging on the wall. J.W. brought in the stench of whiskey, and Emmett, of course, the fear.

Roy handed J.W. the flashlight and went back to keep watch at the door.

"Take off your clothes, nigger!"

J.W. trained the beam of light on Emmett as he quickly peeled himself out of his T-shirt and jeans.

"Your draws too!"

Roy gave his head a pitiful shake and wished that someone would come along and stop this thing.

When Emmett was naked, J.W. ridiculed his penis.

"Roy, you see this? They say niggers got big dicks. Well, his ain't but the size of my pinky finger." He laughed. "Come here, come look at it!"

Roy shook his head. "Nah, that's okay, J.W."

Emmett brought his hands over his genitals and screamed through his sobs. "Shut up already and go on ahead and get it over with!"

Roy was thinking about running. In high school, he had been Roy Bryant, Junior Varsity Track Star. He peered down at his feet and wondered if he still had the speed to outrun a bullet.

"Roy!"

"Yeah?"

"Come and do what we came here for."

Roy wasn't exactly certain what was expected. His eyes swung to Emmett and back to J.W.

"You gotta teach him a lesson!" J.W.'s eyes rolled crazily in their sockets.

Roy sighed and walked slump-shouldered over to the black boy. He balled his hand into a loose fist and socked Emmett in the mouth. The boy groaned and clasped his hand over his bruised lips.

"Again!" J.W. yelled.

Roy struck Emmett hard across the side of his head, and Emmett fell to the ground weeping. Roy turned on his brother. "Okay? You happy now? Let's go home." He dragged his hands through his hair and walked back toward the door.

"You faggot!"

That was a word Roy hated more than

anything. He spun around angrily. "What did you call —" he began, and then realized that his half-brother's taunt was meant for Emmett.

J.W. stood menacingly over Emmett. Not a lick of sympathy shone in his eyes as he watched the boy cry and rock in pain. "You niggers — you niggers make me sick!" he bellowed, and kicked Emmett in the ribs.

Emmett screamed, tried and failed to block the next kick and the one after that. The third one broke two ribs and he slipped into unconsciousness. That's when J.W. went for the hatchet hanging on the wall.

CHAPTER TWENTY-FIVE

When Roy got home, he went out behind the store and burned every piece of clothing he had on, including his shoes. In the shower he stood beneath a steady stream of scalding-hot water until his skin turned pink. When he opened the bathroom door, a cloud of steam followed him out.

In the kitchen he opened the refrigerator and commenced to eat every piece of food it contained.

Carolyn had been standing at the bedroom window when the Buick pulled into the yard and Roy climbed out. She had run outside pelting questions: "What happened? Where you been? What y'all do to that boy?"

If she had not seen Roy climb out that car, she would have thought she was looking at a dead man, because his face was so still and pale.

Roy didn't answer any of her questions, nor did he mumble a word for most of the morning. He had left his voice near the river, and when it finally found him again, it spewed out of his mouth in great, sorrowful wails of regret.

The last time J.W. could remember sleeping as soundly as he did that day was when he was in the war.

He woke in the late hours of the afternoon with the previous night's events scattered through his mind like the remnants of a dream.

He stumbled to the bathroom, and as he stood at the toilet relieving himself, his eyes floated over to the heap of blood-splattered clothes. He began to reel with laughter.

Moe Wright, his wife, Hank, and the other boys sat up all night long waiting for J.W. and Roy to return Emmett. When the sun came up, and Emmett still wasn't home, Moe climbed into his pickup truck and drove down to Bryant's grocery store.

Roy was behind the counter.

"Morning," Moe Wright managed steadily.

"What can I get you, Moe?" Roy said without looking at the old man.

"My boy. My grandnephew."

Roy wished he could go to one of the shelves and pull Emmett from amidst the canned goods, bags of flour, and tins of sardines — if he could do that, he would hand the boy right over to Moe and say, *No charge, Moe.*

Instead, Roy moved to the register and hit the cash sale button. The drawer slid open and he peered down at the money. It was eighteen dollars and seventy-two cents — he knew this because in an effort to wash Emmett's face from his mind he had counted and recounted the money. And now he withdrew it from the drawer and began counting it again.

"Ain't he home?" Roy mumbled as he thumbed through the bills.

"No suh, he ain't."

"Well, I don't know where he could be. We slapped him around some and then put him out just down the road from your house."

Moe knew a lie when he heard one. "Have a good day Mr. Bryant," he said, and walked calmly out of the store.

He went to the sheriff and the sheriff assured him that he would look into the matter. And he did; that very night he questioned J.W. Milam as they sat playing poker.

"Moe Wright says you and Roy took one of his boys out for a whipping and didn't bring him back. Is that true?"

J.W. rolled his cigar from one corner of his mouth to the other. He smoothed his hand over the bald part of his head, but kept his eyes on his cards.

"Yeah, we took him and then brought him back."

"You brought him back to the house?"

"Nah, we let him out down the road some."

"Oh," the sheriff sounded, and then abruptly folded his hand.

Three days later, the Sunday morning sky was splattered with thick clouds when Carson Long woke up determined to get some fishing in before church.

At the river, he cast his line out over the water and sat down on the old wooden crate that doubled as a stool. A breeze rattled the tree limbs and filled Carson's nose with the putrid stench of rotting flesh, causing him to double over and puke up the fine breakfast his wife had made for him.

He dragged his shirttail over his mouth and then used it to cover his nose. Figuring it was a dead animal — possibly a dog — he set out in search of the corpse.

Barely thirty paces away from his fishing spot, Carson came upon a thick swarm of blue bottle flies. He combed his arms through the air and the flies scattered. When he looked down, his stomach lurched again.

He couldn't drive. Not after seeing what he'd just seen. His hands were trembling too badly and his eyes kept tearing up. So he walked to Moe Wright's house on shaky legs.

Moe opened the door and offered Carson a somber good morning. He stepped out onto the porch tugging the straps of his overalls over his shoulders. There were circles beneath his eyes as thick and dark as crude oil.

Carson looked into the man's strained face. If there was another way to say it, an easier way, Carson would have done so, but there wasn't.

"I think I found your boy."

Moe scratched his stomach. "Where?"

"Down by the river."

Moe excused himself and disappeared back into the house. When he returned he was wearing a blue cotton shirt and a brown baseball cap with a picture of an elk on the lid.

"We have to take your truck," Carson said.

When they reached the river, Carson offered his hand to the old man as they descended the short hill that led to that place where the blue bottle flies were feeding.

"That him, ain't it?"

Moe placed the hat over his face. When he spoke, his words were muffled. "I can't be sure."

The clouds parted and a shaft of sunlight beamed straight down onto Emmett's dead body and bounced off the silver ring on his finger.

"Yeah," Moe managed to choke out. "That's him."

Moe Wright went home and called Emmett's mother and she screamed and screamed until he couldn't take it anymore and laid the phone down on his lap.

Tass heard the screen door squeak open and bounce softly closed again.

"I got coffee made," Hemmingway said.

"No, too hot for that. Thanks though."

Silence.

"He dead, ain't he?"

"Yeah."

"Jesus."

"I was the one who found him."

"Mercy," Hemmingway cried, and then, "Where?"

"In the river."

"They butchered that boy. Even Moe Wright wasn't sure it was him, and that's his kin."

"Goddamn crackers!"

"One of his eyes was hanging out . . ."

"Humph."

"Look like they took a butcher knife or something to his nose and across the top of his head —"

"My God, my God!"

"Took it to his private parts too." Carson let off a weary sigh. "Shot him through the temple, tied him to a cotton gin fan, and tossed him in the Tallahatchie."

Hemmingway started to weep.

"Sorry to be the bearer of bad news."

In her bedroom, Tass pushed her face into her pillow and screamed.

CHAPTER TWENTY-SIX

The coroner placed his body into a pine box and sealed it shut. When his mother arrived at the funeral home where they stored the body, they stopped her at the door and informed her that she could not see her dead son and that there was a law that required the body to be buried immediately.

Mamie Till pursed her lips, pulled the handles of her pocketbook up over her shoulder, and left.

Back at Moe's house she called a cousin in Chicago.

"They killed my boy and now they telling me I can't bring him home."

The cousin said, "Sons of bitches! You wait right there by the phone. I'ma call you back."

The cousin knew people in local authority in Illinois and those people knew people in the state legislature. When Moe Wright's telephone rang again, Mamie Till answered.

"Hello?"

"You don't worry, Mamie, things have been set in motion."

At the sheriff's department and in the office of the undertaker, one call after another came in from people neither man had ever heard of.

Some of the callers were cordial; many others were downright nasty. One man threatened, "Heads will roll!" Another promised, "You and your family will be dead by dawn."

When Mamie Till answered the phone early the following morning, it was the undertaker's voice she heard.

"I done already made the arrangements. The casket will be placed on the next train headed to Chicago."

Click.

In Chicago, Mrs. Till placed a call to John H. Johnson, the president and CEO of the Johnson Publishing Company. In 1955, Johnson's *Jet Magazine* had a circulation in the black community that counted in the hundreds of thousands.

Mr. Johnson took the call, and offered his deep and sincere condolences. Mrs. Till thanked him and asked if he wouldn't mind sending a couple of his *Jet Magazine* photographers to her son's funeral.

Johnson was taken off guard by the request and politely asked, "Why would you want me to do that, Mrs. Till?"

There was a pause and then Mamie Till said, "So the world can see what those men down in Mississippi did to my boy."

A broken heart would have been kind, mendable — but Tass's heart was shattered so completely the pieces were small enough to fit through the eye of a needle.

A man leaving a woman was one thing — there was always the possibility of reconciliation. A woman could live months and years on that possibility.

But how does one wait for death to come to an end? Death is final, right? Wrong! Death is the end and the beginning. But I am getting ahead of myself.

Hemmingway and Padagonia didn't know how to make Tass feel happy again, and so they just waited for the melancholy to drift away. But it never did — not really. It faded some, got washed out a bit and worn down in places, but if you looked real hard, you could always see it pulsing behind her eyes.

The September issue of *Jet Magazine* just made things worse. Of course, Bryant's grocery store didn't carry the magazine, so a few people went to Greenwood to buy copies. They brought them back here and passed them around amongst the residents. When folks saw that black-and-white photo of Emmett "Bobo" Till, laid out in a coffin with his face so battered it looked like a Halloween mask, the rage it elicited spread like fever.

Because Moe Wright and his family had witnessed J.W. Milam and Roy Bryant remove Emmett from their house, the law picked the two white men up and put them in jail to await their trial. When their defense attorney told them that they were being charged with murder in the first degree, Roy almost pissed on himself and J.W. laughed.

"Even if we did kill that boy — and we didn't — ain't no court in the land gonna convict two white men for killing a nigger."

At the trial, Carolyn Bryant took the stand and placed her left hand on the Bible and raised her right hand into air and swore to tell the truth, the whole truth, and nothing but the truth.

The defense lawyer asked, "Did Emmett Till whistle at you?"

"Yes sir, he did."

Tass, Hank, and Padagonia were called into testify.

"Did Emmett Till whistle at Carolyn Bryant? Yes or no?"

"He whistled, but —"

"Yes or no!"

"But sir, what I want to say —"

"Your Honor, please instruct this witness to respond to the question with a yes or no."

"Respond to the question with a yes or no."

"I'll ask the question again: on the afternoon of August 24, 1955, did Emmett Till, a.k.a. Bobo, whistle at Carolyn Bryant?"

"Yes sir, he did."

As if having an all-white jury didn't already guarantee their acquittal, the defense went so far as to claim that the body pulled from the Tallahatchie wasn't even Emmett Till, but some cadaver planted by the NAACP. To add insult to injury, they accused Mrs. Till of faking her son's murder to collect a four hundred–dollar death benefit.

A white man who claimed to have seen the body before it was boxed and shipped out of the state said that he was more than sure that it wasn't Emmett Till. When asked why he was so confident in his belief, the man threw his hands up in the air and declared: " 'Cause that body had hair on its chest and everybody knows niggers don't grow no hair on their chest until they're twenty years old!"

On September 23, 1955, less than one month after the day Emmett Till was kidnapped, murdered, and mutilated, Roy Bryant and J.W. Milam were found not guilty and strolled out of the courthouse into the autumn sunshine, free men.

Some people called it one of the worst days in the history of the American judicial system. Others claimed that if Dwight D. Eishenhower, who was the sitting president at that time, had said something — anything that expressed his abhorrence at what those men had done to that boy — things might have turned out different. But Eisenhower didn't say one thing — which led some to believe that maybe he was okay with what J.W. and Roy had done to Emmett Till.

Two months after the men were acquitted of murder, the grand jury declined to indict them on kidnapping charges.

Double jeopardy is a term most people who lived here had not been familiar with before the Till murder, but it became one they would remember for the rest of their lives. In 1956, Bryant and Milam sold their story

to *Look Magazine,* wherein Milam unabash-
edly admitted that he had killed Emmett
Till and didn't feel one iota of remorse.

A confession, printed in black-and-white
in a national publication, and there wasn't
anything any court in the land could do
about it. Milam and Bryant had been found
innocent of murder and could not be trialed
for the same crime twice.

Double jeopardy.

Hemmingway took her distraught daughter
into her arms. "That's man's law, baby.
Man's law don't outweigh God's law. Don't
you worry, they'll get theirs."

And they did.

Even the most racist of Mississippians
didn't condone what Milam and Bryant had
done to Emmett.

The brothers were ostracized by black and
white alike. Friendless, stigmatized, and unable to make a living, the brothers closed
the store and moved their families to Texas
to start new lives.

They could run, but they could not hide.
Their photos had been splashed on the front
pages of every major newspaper in the
country, so they couldn't go anywhere
without being recognized.

In Texas, white people pointed and blared,

"Look at the child killers!"

So misery became as much a part of their lives as oxygen.

A decade later, Milam moved back to Mississippi and took a job as a machinist. He arrived at work on time, performed his duties, and at the end of the day returned home to his whiskey and cigars.

He contemplated suicide, but never had the guts to do it. At night he closed his eyes and prayed for death, but always woke up to a brand-new day.

When they found the cancer in his liver, he refused all treatment that was available to him. He thought that untreated, the end would come quick.

He thought wrong.

J.W. languished in excruciating pain for years.

When he died in 1980, the autopsy revealed that he had tumors in every major organ of his body.

In 1994, at the age of sixty-three, Roy Bryant died of complications from diabetes and liver cancer.

At the telling of this story, Carolyn Bryant was still alive, but not so well.

CHAPTER TWENTY-SEVEN

He was dark-skinned and charming. A twenty-five-year-old dreamer who loved to clown, play cards, and smoke cigars.

His name was Maximillian May, but because he had a passion for fishing, his family and friends had dubbed him Fish.

When he spotted Tass out in front of her house scattering dirt, bits of string, and flower petals with a straw broom, he stopped his car, climbed out, walked right over, and reintroduced himself.

"Tass Hilson, right? You remember me? Fish May?"

Tass looked at his hands and his eyes, and said, "Uh-huh, I remember you. How you been?"

The conversation started there and continued in the house after Hemmingway came out and asked if he would like to stay for a meal.

At the dining table, Fish explained that he

was living in Detroit, working in the salt mines, but waiting on a job at the motor plant to come through.

"I ain't gonna be there long though, gonna work for myself."

"Oh yeah? Doing what?" Hemmingway asked as she scooped a second helping of mashed potatoes onto his plate.

"Real estate."

"Real estate?"

"Yes, ma'am! Buying, selling, and building."

Hemmingway glanced at Tass, who was thoughtfully studying the line of Fish's jaw.

"Building? You know how to build a house?"

"Yes, ma'am! I'm a builder's apprentice."

"Apprentice? What's that?"

"It's like a student."

"Oh. Ain't that something," Hemmingway crooned, and looked at Tass. "Don't you think that's something, Tass?"

"Yes, it is."

After Fish left, Tass helped Hemmingway wash and dry the dinner plates.

"Well, he has certainly grown into a nice young man."

"Uh-huh," Tass mumbled.

"He seems to like you."

"You think so?" Tass asked with an air of disinterest.

"Did you see how he was looking at you?"

"No."

Hemmingway tossed the sponge into the sink and turned sober eyes on her daughter.

"He ain't coming back, Tass."

How many times had her mother said that to her? Too many to count. And each time Hemmingway uttered those words, Tass was reminded of how silly the statement was. Of course he wasn't coming back. He had been dead and buried for two years by then.

Tass was only seventeen and still had a year of school left. Now, seventeen might seem too young for a mother to be pushing her daughter into the arms of an eligible bachelor, but in 1957, in rural Mississippi, with no prospects of ever going to college, but certainly the opportunity to become some white woman's maid, the act was as common as cotton.

Tass reached for the sponge and squeezed it until it was free of every drop of water.

"I know that."

"You gotta move on with your life, Tass."

Tass dropped the sponge back into the sink. "I know, Mama, I know."

Fish courted Tass with all he had. He sent

letters, thin greeting cards painted with smiling cats holding bouquets of flowers, and boxes containing stuffed animals, perfume, and fashion magazines.

He drove from Detroit down to Mississippi twice in four months. On his second visit, Tass allowed him to kiss her, but the dizzying, drunken feeling she'd experienced when she'd kissed Emmett didn't return. Disappointed, her heart began to slip back into hiding.

"He's a fine catch," Hemmingway pushed. "Not one man here in this town can hold a candle to him."

"I know, Mama, I know."

The letters and packages continued to come, and then one day a man from the telephone company knocked on their door and presented Hemmingway with a pink service order.

"I ain't order no telephone," Hemmingway said.

The white man pulled a handkerchief from his pocket and swabbed the perspiration from his forehead, and then snatched the slip of paper from Hemmingway's hand. After scanning it, he said, "Maximillian May," and shoved it back at her.

Hemmingway refused to accept the paper

and folded her arms defiantly across her breasts. At that point she was so angry that she didn't even recognize the name.

"He don't live here!"

"Look, lady, don't give me a hard time about this, okay? Just let me do my job and install the goddamn telephone line."

"I will not!"

The man swabbed his forehead for a second time. "Look, I ain't coming back out here again, you hear me? It's today or never."

Hemmingway eyed him. "Like I said, I ain't order no phone, I ain't got no money for no phone, and so I don't want no phone."

"Look, lady, you ain't got to worry about paying for anything. The person on the order," he said as he shook the paper in her face, "he already done covered that, and he's the one who will pay the monthly charges."

Hemmingway leaned back on one leg. "What name you say was on the order?"

That evening, Hemmingway and Tass sat and stared at the black rotary phone waiting for it to ring.

"This is so nice of him," Hemmingway kept saying. "You see, Tass, I told you he was a good man."

When it finally did ring, both Hemmingway and Tass nearly jumped out of their skin. Tass answered the phone with a meek "Hello," and Fish's jovial voice boomed from the other end.

"I installed this phone for your mama, so you two can talk when I marry you and move you to Detroit."

That was his proposal and Tass, not really caring if she stayed or left, lived or died, said, "Okay."

A month after she graduated and three days after she turned eighteen, Tass Hilson became Tass May.

Remember those ten crisp hundred-dollar bills? Hemmingway used three of them to pay for the wedding. Fancy invitations and a church ceremony, followed by a reception at the colored social hall.

Tass looked lovely in her white, laced, trimmed wedding gown. Instead of a veil, she wore a wreath of pink flowers in her hair. Padagonia was her maid of honor, and although she was not one for dresses, for her friend she happily donned the lilac-colored frock and white panty hose.

Tass asked Moe Wright if he would walk her down the aisle, and he agreed, and broke down in tears when he presented her to Fish.

Tass and Fish jumped the broom and shared a long, hard kiss and guests whooped with joy.

At the social hall, the new couple and their guests danced, ate, and drank until the sun went down.

It was a beautiful day.

When it was time to go, Fish wrapped his arm affectionately around Tass's waist and said, "We gotta get on the road, baby."

"No tears now," Hemmingway warned as she dabbed her own wet eyes with a napkin. "You ain't going to the moon. It's just Detroit."

Fish loaded Tass's belongings into the trunk and climbed into the driver's seat and lit a cigar. In the rearview mirror he watched Hemmingway and Tass clinging to one another and rocking. The mother was the one who finally broke the embrace.

"Oh, I almost forgot," Hemmingway squealed, and clapped her hands. "Wait a minute."

She rushed back into the hall and returned seconds later, carrying a small clay flowerpot filled with dandelions. "It'll be like bringing a little bit of Money to Detroit," she said.

Tass smiled, and reached out and stroked her mother's arm. "Thank you for everything."

In the car, Fish glanced at the pot Tass clutched in her lap and laughed. "That ain't nothing but a weed. We got weeds in Detroit!"

"I know," Tass said as she laid her head on his shoulder. "I know."

And that's how I followed Tass Hilson-May all the way to the Motor City.

CHAPTER TWENTY-EIGHT

Her new home was an old Victorian on a broad street lined with oak trees. Across from the house stood a three-story redbrick hospital.

Tass pointed her finger at the structure and said, "That's convenient. We don't have to go far if we get sick."

"They don't treat colored folk in that hospital, baby."

The neighborhood, once all white, was now speckled with brown families. At first, the whites moved out under cover of night, but now they left in broad daylight, in a steady stream of moving trucks.

The house was a mansion compared to what Tass had grown up in. Two floors, four bedrooms, and one bathroom. A parlor, dining room, and den were packed tight with all manner of things that should have been stored in a garage or toolshed.

The lace curtains covering the windows

were dry rot. At the slightest touch, the lace disintegrated into dust. The wooden floors were black with age and dirt, and the throw rugs riddled with bald spots. Who knew what color the kitchen walls were beneath the layers of grease and grime? Every pot and pan in that house was filled with nuts, bolts, screws, and nails, and the kitchen sink was piled high with dirty dishes sprouting mold.

"I know," Fish stammered when he saw the astonished look on Tass's face. "It's a mess, but I'm sure you'll have this house spotless in a day or two."

Tass stared at him like he'd lost his mind. "Maybe you should have hired a maid instead of taking a wife."

The first time Tass saw snow was on May 16, 1957, just two days after she'd arrived in Detroit. The sight of it was accompanied by thunder that clapped and marched across the sky, and fork lightning.

The snow began to fall an hour after the orchestra of *BOOM — BANG — Brrrr-RUMMM* drove people off the streets and into the safety of their homes. It came down soft, like tufts of cotton, and covered everything. It laid white sheets over the rooftops and the high school football field. It clasped hold to tree limbs, coated cars like flour, and sugared the daffodils and tulips.

Harsh winds swept the snow into molehills and mountains that blocked doorways and driveways. In a matter of hours Detroit was buried beneath twelve inches of late-spring snow and Tass was left wondering just how she would manage — newly arrived from the sweltering state of Mississippi without galoshes, winter coat, knit hat, or mittens.

She had set the clay flowerpot on the windowsill and now she stood there staring at the yellow blooms against the bright white of the snow and began to long for the time before that moment, when she wasn't a wife — just Tass Hilson, daughter of Hemmingway Hilson, best friend to Padagonia Tucker, and fool in love for the first time in her life.

"What you doing, huh?" Fish called from their bed. "Come on, Tass, ole boy ain't had his fill yet."

She looked over her shoulder to see her husband waving his dick like a kid with a flag at an Arbor Day parade.

When it rained, the roof would leak and Tass would sob.

Pails, pots, and bowls were set out to catch the water. Tass caught her tears in napkins and spilled sick into the toilet. Her breasts swelled and her nipples started to look like water plugs. The scent of cooking meat turned her stomach. Her feet expanded like dough. The cravings for ice cream and salted peanuts nearly drove her out of her mind.

Tass called her mother and explained, "I'm gonna have a baby."

And Hemmingway replied, "Awww, that's nice."

It was midnight when the first pain struck low in her womb, and Tass sat straight up in bed. Fish was across town, playing poker with friends. The second pain grew fingers that grabbed hold of her uterus and squeezed. Tass howled, stumbled out of the house and over to her neighbors. She banged on the door until her water broke.

The third pain balled its fist and punched her in the back, and Tass yanked a patch of hair from her scalp and nearly bit through her tongue. She waddled across the street and into the hospital that didn't cater to coloreds.

Her bare feet slapped noisily across the marble floor of the brightly lit lobby. The nurse at the receiving desk blanched when she saw Tass coming toward her, panting and clutching a tuft of kinky hair in her hand.

"H-help me," Tass yelped.

The woman opened and then closed her mouth.

The fourth contraction brought Tass down to her knees.

The nurse finally found her words and they spewed like sewage from her mouth: "Noooooooo niiiiiggers!"

Tass rolled onto her back, raised her knees, and began to push. When she screamed, the nurse threw her hands into the air and screamed too.

The first colored child ever to be born in that hospital was a big-head boy with dreamy eyes. They named him Maximillian May the second, but called him Sonny.

The hospital closed down a year later, relocated the staff, sold off the equipment, and boarded up the windows.

Drug addicts used crowbars to peel back the wood, climbed in, and gutted the building of everything they could sell. After that, someone set fire to the structure and the city bulldozed the remains and carted them away.

Now it's an empty lot where people dump their garbage and winos gather over campfires to sing old songs.

Three months after Sonny was born, the familiar cravings started again. The morning sickness wasn't as bad, and the rain didn't make her quite so sad . . . They named the second boy James.

For a time Tass was a factory, similar to Chrysler and Ford, churning out a new model of baby every year. She and Fish would go on to produce a baker's dozen by 1970.

The frequency with which she became pregnant made Tass feel a little bit ashamed. Hemmingway didn't help alleviate those feelings; in fact, she added to them. When Tass called to tell her mother that she was pregnant for the sixth time in just as many years, the silence her announcement was met with was devastating.

"Mama, did you hear me?"

Hemmingway sighed, "Yeah, I heard you, Tass. Well, I guess congratulations are in order . . . again."

A wounded Tass replied, "Okay, Mama, I'll call you next week," and put down the phone without even a goodbye.

Every year, Hemmingway spent Thanksgiving through to New Years with Tass and her family. In September of 1967, Tass gave birth to a little girl named Debra. She didn't mention the pregnancy or the arrival of the child to Hemmingway; she just couldn't bear to hear that tone in Hemmingway's voice, or the disingenuous *congratulations*.

Two days before Thanksgiving that year, Fish collected Hemmingway from the bus depot. In the house, Hemmingway greeted her daughter and brood of grandchildren with smiles, kisses, and hugs.

She took a seat at the dining room table and Tass brought her a cup of coffee and a pecan roll. Upstairs, the new baby, closed away in Tass's bedroom, began to wail. Her cries crept through the heating vent and seeped out into the dining room.

Hemmingway set her cup down, cocked her head to one side, and listened. Then she shot Tass a sharp look and said, "Jesus, girl, can't you keep your legs closed?"

What occurred between Hemmingway's visits and the delivering of babies was croup, evening prayers, diarrhea, colds, ear infections, pink eye, broken arms, parent-teacher nights, mumps, skinned knees, measles, chicken pox, first day of school, gold-starred reports, failing marks, whippings, kisses, last day of school, and summer vacation.

For many years, Tass's life was like an echo.

Chapter Twenty-Nine

There were kind years and hard years. Long periods that found Tass and her family living from pillar to post. Months when there was barely enough money to buy beans and flour. One winter, they couldn't afford to fill the oil tank and spent the entire season huddled together in two rooms kept warm by kerosene heaters.

When Hemmingway slipped softly away during one of the hard years, Fish's employer advanced him his pay, which was just enough to buy bus tickets for Tass and Sonny to go down and attend to things.

Padagonia met them at the bus depot and Tass was surprised at how hard-in-the-face she looked. Tass hadn't seen Padagonia since she'd given birth to her second child back in 1959. Considering how poor their finances were, it just made more sense for them to bring Hemmingway up north. Tass had invited Padagonia to come and visit numerous times, and she always said that she would, but never did.

Padagonia was wearing a checkered long-sleeve shirt, baggy denims, hunting boots, and a baseball cap. She looked more like a man than a woman and Tass had to pinch Sonny when he whispered under his breath, "Is she a dyke, Mama?"

"No," Tass hissed unsurely.

The two old friends threw their arms around each other. Tass winced; being hugged by Padagonia was like being clasped by a wire hanger.

"You need to put some meat on those bones, girl!" Tass teased. "This is Sonny, my oldest boy."

Sonny offered his hand and Padagonia took it and shook it like a man.

"Wow, last time I saw you, you were just a little tot. Now look at you, all grown up!"

Sonny grinned.

Padagonia brought her face close to his and exclaimed, "My goodness, Tass, do you know this boy got hair growing above his lip?"

Sonny blushed with embarrassment.

The funeral was small. Most of the people who had known Tass and Hemmingway had either died or moved away.

At the cemetery, Sonny couldn't stop fidgeting. Graveyards gave him the willies, so when the coffin was lowered into the ground, Sonny excused himself and double-timed it out to the street, where he waited with Padagonia who was puffing on a black and tan, with one foot cocked up on the fender of her silver Pacer.

Tass lingered. Nearby were the graves of her uncle and the grandparents she never knew. The tombstones had begun to sink and tilt, but the names and dates on the stones were as legible as they had been the day they were etched.

"I guess I'm officially an orphan now," Tass murmured to the air as a lone tear trickled down her cheek.

Hemmingway had never revealed the identity of Tass's father, and the one time Tass did ask, her mother had responded sharply, "I'm your mother *and* your father."

When Tass was ten years old, she and Padagonia had spent an entire summer searching for her face in those of the men around town. The two spent hours sitting outside of Bryant's grocery store, scrutinizing the faces of the men who trailed in and out of the store. This went on until someone reported back to Hemmingway: "That child of yor'n and her friend down by the store

eyeballing people like it's nobody's business. They keep it up and somebody gonna
take a switch to their behinds."

Tass wiped her eyes and chuckled at the
memory.

As she continued reminiscing, she was
suddenly overcome with the feeling that she
was being watched. She turned and saw a
crew of gravediggers milling about, obviously waiting for her to leave. So she started
across the lawn and walked right into a spi-
derweb, or at least what felt like a spider-
web. She was swiping at her face when she
felt the unmistakable tickle of a feather in
her ear, followed by a gentle breath of air
against her cheek. Little did she know that
the lines of communication between the
here-and-now and the beyond were now
open.

Yes, Emmett's body was buried in Illinois,
but his spirit had remained here with me.
Why? Because this was where the last good
thing happened.

Did you forget the kiss?

What do you think he was dreaming about
when those men came and dragged him out
his bed?

In his dream, the road stretched out for
endless miles and he and Tass walked for
days beneath a clear blue sky. Their ice pops

never melted and Tass planted a kiss on his lips each time they came upon a bend in the road.

There were many, many bends in the road.

Dearest, you must understand that crossing over to the other side is the same as drifting off to sleep. One full day for you is an entire year for a soul.

When Emmett had finally opened his eyes in the here-and-now, he found that his body was no more, that the boys he'd known were now men and the girls had blossomed into women. Tass was gone and Hemmingway was graying around her hairline.

He went first to the home of Moe Wright, but found only a dry tract of land where the house once stood. The next place he went was to Hemmingway Hilson's house. He took up residence on her porch, where he remained for many years.

When Hemmingway died, her spirit came to him and said, "I figured that was you." She looked off into the distance and then back at him and added, "She'll be here soon." And then skipped away into the blue.

Emmett had watched Padagonia step out of her house, cross the road, and knock on the door, calling, "Miss Hemmingway?"

When she did not receive an answer, she had gone to the window and pressed her face against the glass. Finally, she picked up the one lone flowerpot on the porch and removed the key hidden beneath it.

Moments after she let herself inside of the house, Emmett heard her gasp. When Padagonia reappeared, she had tears in her eyes.

Days later, when Tass and her son arrived, Emmett had sensed her presence as soon as she stepped off the bus. He was happy to feel himself in her thoughts and glad to know that she hadn't forgotten about him.

But I ask you, dear reader, how could she forget him? How could she possibly forget, when year after year August 28 rolled around and *Jet Magazine* republished that horrid photo, reminding Tass and the rest of the world of what had happened here during the summer of 1955?

And what of the murder of Medgar Evers in Jackson, Mississippi, in 1963? And the following year, in Philadelphia, Mississippi, where three civil rights workers were beaten, shot to death, and buried in a field?

Those murders always brought Emmett Till back to the forefront of not just Tass's mind, but the minds of many people all around the world.

Tass's heart raced and her body tensed as

she launched into a sprint. When she reached the street, she was trembling and her eyes were wild with fear.

"Mama, what's wrong?" Sonny asked.

"You okay?" Padagonia took hold of her hand and squeezed.

"I'm fine. Just fine," Tass stammered. "Let's go home."

The house seemed even smaller than she remembered. The ceiling was so low, Sonny had to walk stooped over through the rooms.

Together they carried out the task of sorting through, throwing out, and giving away Hemmingway's scant possessions. They got rid of everything except for the beds, a dresser, and a rocking chair.

That evening, Padagonia and Tass sat on the porch and gazed up at the star-filled sky.

"You gonna sell the place?" Padagonia asked.

"Maybe."

"Well then," Padagonia offered with a gentle pat to Tass's thigh, "I'll keep an eye on it till you decide."

Sonny and Tass boarded a bus headed north just four days after they arrived. Padagonia was sad to see them go and promised that she would come soon for a visit. Tass laughed and said, "I won't hold my breath."

Emmett floated on board and rode on Tass's lap all the way to Detroit.

CHAPTER THIRTY

November through March had always been particularly difficult months for Tass. Detroit was beautiful in the spring, gorgeous in the summer, and breathtaking in the fall. But stripped and gray, the city became repulsive.

In the early days, when Emmett first came to Detroit, he would send a butterfly or bloom a flower to make her happy. A smile would glisten on Tass's lips and she would fold her arms across her breasts and utter, "Well, would you look at that."

Unfortunately, the wonderment did not last and soon the spectacle would fade from her mind.

One January, slate-colored clouds blanketed the sky over Detroit for three straight weeks, and while Tass had grown accustomed to the bone-chilling temperatures, the absence of the sun was nearly unbearable.

262

Tass was alone in the house dusting furniture one day, and for no good reason at all, she began to cry. Crumpling to her knees, she brought the dusty cloth to her face and inhaled a cloud of lemon-scented Pledge.

Over her sobs, she heard a chorus of chirping coming from the backyard. Baffled, Tass went to the window, yanked the curtain aside, and saw that the naked tree limbs were choked with hundreds of cardinals feathered in the most vibrant red she had ever seen.

Eager for a closer look, she opened the back door and stepped out onto the icy steps. Outside, the chatter was deafening and the vision so magnificently unbelievable that she presumed she was in the midst of an outlandish daydream.

Closing her arms around her shoulders to ward off the chill, she eased her foot onto the second step, immediately lost her footing, and bounced down the remaining steps, ending up on her back in the snow.

Engrossed by the vision before her, Tass hardly noticed the pain coiling around her tailbone or winter's jagged teeth ripping at her skin.

One bird, two birds, five, and ten fluttered off, then the entire flock was airborne, and for one magical moment the winter sky appeared to be swathed in crimson-colored Christmas foil.

When you are young, you are open to all things; that's why the babies were able to see Emmett following Tass from room to room, and hunched in the corners watching her. Emmett would make funny faces at the babies and perform cartwheels and handstands until they fell over with laughter.

But as the babies grew into toddlers and beyond, that window known as spiritual consciousness slipped closed and Emmett became as invisible to them as air.

Animals are also extremely sensitive to the spirits that live amongst you.

Fish had to get rid of one of the family dogs, a cocker spaniel named Soap, who found Emmett's presence so disturbing that he barked himself hoarse. A hamster named George mounted his exercise wheel and ran until his heart gave out.

In 1978, Sonny brought his sweetheart by to meet his parents. She was from Ghana.

"Where is that?" Tass asked.

"Africa."

The entire family came over to look at her. They had never met a real African.

Her name was Aida, and she was tall and brown, with wide eyes and cheekbones worthy of a sculptor's chisel. Hearing her speak was like listening to music.

I noticed the distraction first, and then Sonny saw that she was straining to glimpse something on the far wall. He twisted around in his chair to see what had caught her attention and his eyes fell on the framed photographs that lined the wall.

At the end of the visit, Sonny announced that he and Aida were going to catch a movie. The couple gathered themselves to leave and the family followed them out into the foyer and grinned as Sonny helped Aida with her coat.

They said their goodbyes and left.

"Nice girl," Tass said.

"Pretty too," Fish added with a wink.

The doorbell rang, and when one of the younger children opened the door, Aida was standing there.

"I forgot my pocketbook."

She walked back into the dining room and reached for the purse, which was dangling on the back of a chair. Before turning to leave, she looked right at Emmett and offered a soft, knowing smile.

Emmett gasped with surprise.

■ ■ ■ ■

Later on, in the darkness of the movie theater, Sonny and Aida shared a large tub of buttered popcorn. On the screen, Pam Grier pulled a gun on her would-be murderer and pressed the nozzle into his groin.

Aida stared at the screen, but her mind was on the spirit in the May home. She reached for her cup of Coca-Cola and slurped until the brown sweetness filled her mouth.

For most of the film, she pondered whether or not she should share what she knew with Sonny. Finally, when the credits began to roll, she turned to him and whispered, "Do you believe in ghosts?"

Sonny laughed. "No, why, do you?"

Aida nodded her head yes.

He shrugged his shoulders and said, "I guess to each its own," then stood to leave. Aida followed him out of the theater.

As they walked down the street, Aida grabbed hold of his hand and began: "Well, the reason why I asked is because . . ." She launched passionately into her explanation, using her free hand in an animated way to describe what she had seen.

Sonny first thought Aida was joking, but

the seriousness in her voice told him otherwise.

When she was done, he looked her and blurted out with a laugh, "A ghost? In my mama's house?"

"Yes."

He'd had crazy in his life before, and was not eager to invite it back in.

When he dropped Aida off at her home that evening, he shook her hand at the front door. Aida knew then that he didn't believe one word she'd said and that she would never see him again.

CHAPTER THIRTY-ONE

They were thirty years into their marriage when Fish's sight began to fail.

Diabetes.

It was bound to happen. You can't escape a disease like that if you drink Coca-Cola with your breakfast, lunch, and dinner.

Tass had to inject the insulin into his veins, because he couldn't bear to stick himself.

They now had grown children and grandchildren who owned cars and lived close by, but they had their own jobs and families, and not much time to chauffer Fish and Tass around. And so after an entire lifetime of being a passenger, Tass decided she would learn how to drive.

Sonny was recruited to teach her. Fish supervised from the backseat.

Sonny pointed to the pedals. "Okay, Mama. That one is the gas and that one is the brake." He handed her the ignition key.

"Push it in, press down on the brake, and turn the key."

Tass did as she was told and the car roared to life. The younger children watched silently from the porch.

"Now," Sonny said, "shift the gear into dri—"

"See, already you telling her wrong!" Fish barked. Sonny turned around to meet his father's angry eyes.

"How am I telling her wrong, Fish?"

"Did you tell her what the gearshift was?"

Tass was gripping the wheel so tightly her fingers went numb. Her eyes were glued to the wide, open street before her, and when she spoke, the words came from the corner of her mouth: "I know where the gearshift is. I put it in drive, right?"

"Yeah, Mama."

Tass grabbed hold of the gearshift. "How do I know when it's in drive?"

Sonny leaned over and tapped the arched glass embedded in the dashboard.

"*D* is for drive," Fish grumbled.

Tass ignored him. "Do I keep my foot on the brake?"

"Yep!"

She pulled the gear down and watched as the dial clicked to *D*.

"Okay, now ease your foot off the brake

and step on the gas —"

"Gently!" Fish yelled.

The car jerked, Tass shrieked and slammed both feet down on the brake.

Sonny sighed. "Okay, Mama, let's try it once more. This time, keep your foot on the gas."

"Okay."

Tass eased her foot off the brake again and placed it on the gas pedal. She gave it a little pressure and the car began to roll forward. A cheer went up from the children.

The car inched along at a turtle's pace until it reached the corner. Tass stepped down on the brake and looked at Sonny.

"Which way should I go?"

"Whichever way you want."

Fish let off a long, loud yawn. "Left."

Sonny placed his hand over Tass's and together they steered the car left.

"It turned, it turned!" Tass squealed with joy.

"Imagine that," Fish muttered.

A year after Tass learned to drive, Fish suffered a stroke, rendering his left arm and leg useless, and slurring his speech.

At the hospital, Tass and the children cornered Fish's doctor and pelted him with dozens of questions, including the one that was the most difficult to ask: "He still got his mind?"

"Yes." The doctor's response was emphatic. "Luckily, he only suffered some physical fallout, but his mind is still as sharp as it was before the stroke."

Understandably, Fish was frustrated and angry at how his body had turned on him. No soft or comforting words from his wife could expunge the indignation he experienced every time she had to assist him with the handling of his own penis or bend him over the toilet to clean his behind.

The constant humiliation ravaged his ego and Fish began to turn mean.

At first Tass ignored the way he watched her, pointedly and premeditatively. She began to feel like an unwitting target caught in the crosshairs of a sniper's gun.

Fish would go days without speaking to her. For a while he wouldn't eat anything she prepared. The daughters had to bring him casseroles of food and spoon-feed him.

Once, while Tass was outside sweeping dead leaves from the sidewalk, Fish hobbled to the door and locked it. Through the window she could see him sitting in the kitchen, stone-faced and staring. It was nearly dark when one of the children happened to drive by and saw Tass waiting there on the porch. After that incident, Tass had an extra key made which she hid beneath a smiling gnome in the front garden.

The worst act of insolence took place on a crisp, April morning. Fish was sitting at the kitchen table, wrapped in his thick green house robe. The radiators were clanging and whistling as Tass stood at the stove preparing his breakfast.

Fish had been hearing things. Whispers, giggles, feet scrambling up and down the staircase, doors opening and closing, the squeal of bedsprings. He assumed that Tass was slipping men into the house after she put him to bed.

Of course, that was absolutely untrue as Tass was completely devoted to Fish.

Let me explain why he was hearing these things. I know you are familiar with the adage: *Once a man, twice a child.* The words hold more truth than many of you will believe. Remember when I told you that little children are able to see the spirits around them? Well, when a soul begins to slip from the binds of the physical world, the consciousness reverts to its natural state and once again it becomes open and receptive to the spirits that live amongst the host body. For some, the transition has been problematic, which has led to sane people being medicated or institutionalized.

This particular morning, Fish slammed his fist against the table and barked, "You better not be bringing no niggers in my house!"

"Uh-huh," Tass sounded, and kept right on whipping the eggs and turning the bacon.

"What type of woman is you? Imagine, at your age picking up a Jody, and after all I done for you!"

She had grown used to the accusations. It was becoming as customary as her morning cup of coffee.

"You hear me talking to you, Tass?" Again, he brought his fist down hard onto the table.

"Uh-huh," Tass said absently.

Fish was suddenly seized with a pure and toxic rage that propelled his frail body from his chair, into the air, and onto Tass's back. They went down like anchors, tossed into the sea.

On the floor they battled like hellions, until Tass was finally able to free herself and jump to her feet. Backing away from him, she reached for the knife lying in the sink.

"Nigger, don't you ever put your hands on her again. Don't you know I will kill you?"

Not her words, but his. Not her voice,

his voice.

In that moment, Emmett discovered that his love for Tass far exceeded the power to manipulate butterflies, flowers, and birds.

The color drained from Fish's face and the knife slipped from Tass's hand and clattered back into the sink. Husband and wife stared at one another in astonishment, before cautiously casting their gazes around the room.

As far as they could tell, they were alone.

Tass thought it was an oddity, like a person born with one blue eye and one brown eye, or poor black people hitting the lottery two drawings in a row. There was no other way to explain it.

After the moment had passed, Tass reached down to help Fish to his feet, but he was spooked and scrambled across the yellow and brown linoleum with the agility and speed of a lizard.

"Don't touch me," he slurred through his crooked lips.

"Don't be silly," Tass said as she reached for him again.

Fish batted her hands away. "Get off me, you possessed bitch!"

Tass reeled back in surprise. Even during their most horrendous disagreements, Fish had never called her out of her name.

Chapter Thirty-Two

Months after that incident, Tass was in the basement one morning, loading the washing machine with clothes. Fish was in the kitchen finishing his breakfast, excited about the day he and the family were going to spend on Belle Isle. He was eager to see the boats coasting across the water with their white sails flapping in the wind.

He was smiling at the thought when death closed its dark hand over his heart.

Downstairs, the roar of the washing machine masked the sound of Fish's body tumbling from the chair to the floor. So when Tass stepped into the sun-drenched kitchen and saw him stretched out with his good hand clutched to his chest, her heart jumped into her throat.

His eyes were open and a glistening stream of saliva spilled ominously from the corner of his mouth. He was still smiling, not because of the vision he'd conjured of Belle

Isle, but because his people were there. All of the family and friends who had transitioned ahead of him had encircled him, and were weaving his name into an ancient chant.

Fish's foot began to bounce to the rhythm of the song, and he was consumed by a tenderness he had never felt before.

Standing just outside of the circle of ancestors was a person who Fish did not recognize. "Who you?" he asked.

Tass was now on the floor cradling his head in her lap, stroking his cheeks and weeping all over him. "It's me, baby. Tass."

His head lolled to one side and he was gone.

Tass sat there for a long time, holding him, stroking his arms and running her fingers through his hair.

She didn't know how long the telephone had been ringing before she finally heard it. Pulling herself up from the floor and carefully stepping around Fish's body, she picked up the receiver.

"Hello?" Tass sniffed.

"Hey, Mama," Sonny's voice rang from the opposite end of the line. "I'm headed over now. Y'all ready?"

Pulling the coiled telephone cord as far as it would allow, she stepped out into the hallway, cupped her hand over mouth, and whispered, "He gone, Sonny, he gone," as if trying to keep the truth from the dead man himself.

Other than the sound of the clock and Tass's own steady breathing, the house was quiet. The funeral had ended hours ago, but Tass was still dressed in her black skirt suit and pillbox hat with the studded veil. Sitting on the corner of the bed, she leaned forward and folded her hands into her lap. For a long time she just sat there staring at her hands, contemplating the soft wrinkles and brown blemishes. How smooth and pretty her skin had been when she said, *I do,* forty-eight years earlier.

"Forty-eight years," she said aloud.

Now, looking back, she realized that forty-eight years had run off like water.

"Not when we were living it though," Tass chuckled. "There were some days when I didn't think we were gonna make it."

She glanced over her shoulder at Fish's side of the bed, then reached her hand around and patted the place where his feet would have been.

"But we did," she sighed.

CHAPTER THIRTY-THREE

May filtered into June and then spilled out into a July that marked one of the hottest on record. By the time August blinked its bleary eyes, Tass had made up her mind to go back home and sell her mother's house.

She and Sonny were in the attic fishing through a steamer trunk filled with old records, toys, magazines, and photographs. They'd been at it for most of the morning, and there seemed to be no end in sight.

When Sonny stood up and swiped the back of his hand across his forehead in frustration, Tass blurted out the thought that had been pressed onto her tongue for two full weeks.

"I'm going to go down to Money for a while."

Sonny reached into the trunk and pulled out a dusty, dingy Raggedy Ann doll.

"Why? Ain't nobody left down there."

"Padagonia is there."

Sonny held the doll up to the light to study its freckled fabric face.

"That's true, don't know how I could forget her," he chuckled. "I think you could use some time away, and I'm sure Miss Padagonia would enjoy having you around."

Sonny tossed the doll onto the pile designated as garbage.

"Well, Mama," he said as he slipped his hands back into the steamer trunk, "just let me know when you want to go and I'll book your plane ticket."

Tass glanced at her son, who looked so much like his father, and she began to slowly shake her head from side to side. "No, no plane ticket."

Sonny shrugged his shoulders. "Okay, a bus ticket then. Why in the world anyone would want to spend a thousand hours on a bus is . . ." His voice trailed off. When it returned it was bursting with excitement. "My old baseball mitt!"

He tried in vain to fit the childhood glove onto his grown-man hand.

"Not the bus either," Tass said.

Sonny struggled for a few more seconds and then tossed the mitt aside. "Aww, man, it don't fit. Well, I'll give it to one of my boys."

Tass laughed. "Those sons of yours ain't a

bit interested in playing baseball. All they interested in is that Internet."

Sonny chuckled in agreement and then he finally heard what Tass had said. "Wait. Not the bus? So what, the train?"

Tass shook her head no again.

"So how you expect to get there?"

"In the car."

Sonny eyed her. "Aw, c'mon, Mama," he whined. "That's a long-ass drive. I ain't got any more time to —"

Tass raised her hand. "I'm not asking you to drive me anywhere, Sonny."

"Well, who then?"

Tass's response was calm and confident: "I'm going to drive myself."

Sonny stared at her for a moment and then started to laugh. "You're joking, right?"

Again Tass shook her head.

"You've only ever driven the same twenty or thirty blocks, and to get to Mississippi you have to get on the highway — a number of highways — and you have never driven on one."

"Gotta learn sometime."

Quiet amazement spread across Sonny's face. "You're serious, aren't you?"

"Yep."

The second reel of laughter doubled him over. When he was finally able to compose himself, he said, "Well, it's not going to happen. I can't let you do it. I've already lost one parent and I'm not ready to bury another."

Tass smirked. "I ain't never known my daddy and your daddy is dead. So the only person who is the boss of me is me."

What was he to do? Yell, scream, bound and gag her until she came to her senses? In the end, he stormed out of the attic, down the stairs, and into the dining room where his sisters were setting the table for dinner.

"Y'all better go up there and talk some sense into your mother!"

"Why, what happened?"

"She talking about driving herself down to Money, Mississippi!"

Up in the attic Tass continued going through the steamer trunk. Taking a break, she walked over to the window and looked out over the backyard. The grass was turning brown from the strangling heat and even though it was only August, fallen leaves were scattered everywhere.

A sparrow landed on the windowsill and gazed curiously at her.

"What you looking at?" Tass quipped.

The bird fluttered off.

After months of melancholy, Tass finally

felt some sense of joy begin to thread through her.

Maybe it was the thought of going home, or just the effect of summer's last stand — whatever it was, Tass was grateful.

CHAPTER THIRTY-FOUR

Peak conditions. That's what the weather-man said. Peak conditions and no rain for at least seven days.

Tass took that uninterrupted perfection as confirmation that it was time to go.

The children pouted.

Of course it was going to be difficult for them — her leaving so soon after Fish had died.

"We're going to feel like orphans," Sonny half-joked.

Tass patted his hand. "You'll be okay. You will all be okay."

She pulled out at sunrise. All twelve children came to see her off. They hugged and kissed her and reminded her not to talk on her cell phone while she was driving.

Sonny typed in the destination on the GPS. The digital numbers stated that she would travel 2,345 miles from point A to point B. When Tass looked at that long number, it took her breath away.

Seat belt in place, she threw the almost-new Toyota into drive and forced a confident smile as she pulled away from the curb.

After twenty miles or so, Tass thought she would turn the car around and head back home. What was she thinking? Who was she fooling? She was a sixty-six-year-old woman who had never spent a night alone in her entire life. This adventure was for a woman half her age, not someone collecting a Social Security check.

Tass began to shake.

Who had put such a silly thought in her mind?

Her eyes filled with tears.

That's it, she belittled herself, *I've lost my mind and not one of my children noticed.*

She frantically searched the overhead signs for the next highway exit. Too nervous and distraught to take her hand off of the steering wheel to turn on the radio, Tass forced herself to think warm and happy thoughts.

She started with the day in the attic, worked her way backward to family barbecues, the birth of her first grandchild, her fortieth anniversary party, the day she and Fish made the final payment on the mortgage, the hour when she first realized she was pregnant, her wedding, summer days at the river, her first kiss . . .

Time slipped by, and before Tass realized it she had traveled fifty miles.

There was still time to turn back, but she no longer felt the urgent need to. Easing her hand from the steering wheel, she fiddled with the buttons until the radio came on. Otis Redding's "Sittin' on the Dock of the Bay" washed over her.

Tass began to sing along.

It was August 22, 2005.

It took her four days to travel the 2,345 miles. She kept to the speed limit, and stopped often, and called Sonny to give him her exact location.

Sonny would always end the phone call with, "I can't believe you're doing this."

And Tass would respond, "I can't believe it either."

She always started driving at dawn, and by sunset she was pulling into a motel to bed down for the night. The rooms at the motels were small, the walls thin, and the cleanliness of the sheets suspect. So Tass slept in her clothes and kept the television on for company.

CHAPTER THIRTY-FIVE

She arrived on the afternoon of August 26. The Toyota was caked in road dust and dead insects. Tass didn't look much better.

After she climbed out of the car, she thanked God for her safe arrival and leaned her entire body against the side of the vehicle.

"Hey, hey, hey!" Padagonia shrieked merrily as she ran out of her house and across the road to Tass. "You made it! Oh, thank God!" Padagonia threw herself into her friend and wrapped her bony arms around her neck.

When they finally pulled apart, Tass smirked and said, "So you knew I was coming, huh?"

Padagonia offered a sheepish grin. "Sonny called me."

"That boy," Tass sighed.

"What did you expect? An old woman like you driving halfway across the country?"

"Old?"

The two laughed.

"Well, make yourself useful," Tass said as she walked around to the back of the car and opened the trunk.

Inside, the house was filled with shadows. Tass's hand crept along the wall in search of the light switch.

"Gosh," she exclaimed, "what's that smell?"

"I painted," Padagonia announced.

Tass hit the switch and the bright light illuminated the pale yellow walls.

"Kinda like a welcome-home present," Padagonia said when Tass turned an astonished gaze on her. "It was depressing, now it's cheery, don't you think?"

Tass nodded. "Yes, it is cheery. Thank you, Paddy."

They hauled the suitcases into the house, down the hall, past Hemmingway's bedroom, and into Tass's room.

"Why don't you sleep in your mama's room, it's bigger," Padagonia suggested.

"No, she died in that room . . . in that bed. I just can't."

"I understand."

Tass walked through the house; there wasn't a speck of dust anywhere. "You

287

cleaned too?"

"Yeah, I just hit it a lick and promised it one," Padagonia chuckled.

"This is too much, Padagonia."

"I didn't mind at all. This is what friends do for one another."

They stepped out onto the porch.

"So what's for dinner?" Tass asked as she looped her arm affectionately around her friend's waist.

"Fried catfish and tater salad."

"That sounds wonderful. I've gotta call the kids to let them know I made it here safely and then I'll come over."

At dinner, fatigue swooped down on Tass and she nodded off at the table.

"Go on home, sleepy-head," Padagonia laughed, and pointed her fork at the door.

Tass's eyes rolled open and a drowsy smile spread across her lips. "Sorry," she managed through a yawn. "Tomorrow then?"

"Tomorrow."

After a short lukewarm shower, Tass slipped on a flannel nightgown, wrapped herself in a quilt, and shuffled back out into the front room. Through the window, she could see Padagonia sitting on her porch, a six-pack of Pink Champale resting on the windowsill alongside her transistor radio.

She was puffing on a black and tan, gazing up at the full moon.

Suddenly, Tass didn't feel as tired and so she moved the rocking chair to the center of living room, sat down, and listened to Padagonia croon along to the music streaming from her radio.

When she woke the next morning, her entire body pulsated with the aches and pains that come along with spending a night in a wooden rocking chair.

The sun was up and there was activity on the street. She could hear a washing machine churning, the colicky cry of a teething infant, and the mournful howl of a chained dog.

Tass limped over to the window and pulled back the curtain. Padagonia was up, dressed, and muttering to herself as she frantically swept the front walk. Every so often, she would whip her entire body around and glare at the emptiness behind her.

Tass frowned and moved to another window to see what or who was irritating her friend. But the only thing that came into view was the weed-choked vacant lot alongside Padagonia's house.

Tass was about to walk away when

Padagonia swung around again and hollered, "Hey! Hey, you in there!"

The tall grass shuddered and laughter floated out.

"Kids," Padagonia mumbled miserably. "Y'all better come out from in there! That grass is filled with snakes and rats and God knows what else!"

The laughter continued.

Padagonia rolled her eyes, sucked her teeth, and returned to her furious sweeping.

Chapter Thirty-Six

Tass stepped out onto the porch and nearly slaughtered the bouquet of wild flowers someone had placed in the doorway.

She uttered a sorrowful "Oh," and bent to retrieve the gift. Of course she thought Padagonia had put them there. But when she walked across the road to thank her, Padagonia gave her a strange look.

"Is it your birthday?"

Tass shook her head.

"Then why would I give you flowers?"

Tass blushed. "But who else?"

Padagonia shrugged her shoulders. "I don't know."

Tass scanned the row of houses on either side of the street.

"Maybe you have a secret admirer," Padagonia suggested.

Tass considered the flowers and then decided she couldn't spend time trying to figure out the who or the why. "I need to go get some food. Come along and give me some company."

Padagonia insisted on driving her weathered, beaten Pacer. The shocks were shot and Tass swore she could feel every groove, pebble, and pothole the road offered. The radio was on and the broadcaster was talking about a tropical depression forming over the Bahamas.

"I sure would like to go there one day," Tass commented.

"Where?"

Tass pointed at the radio. "Where he said. The Bahamas."

They drove happily along until the store came into view and snatched the merriment out of that car.

Tass tried to look away, but couldn't. With her eyes glued to the store she hissed, "Why'd you have to come this way?"

"Because this is the way to the Piggly Wiggly."

Fifty years later and Bryant's grocery store was still standing. Vacant and ghostly, it had survived high winds and treacherous storms, holding onto a life that no longer wanted it — it slouched there, plastered with advertisements and riddled with racial epithets, Bible verses, and swastikas. It stood as a reminder of the then and the now; refusing to die, it clung stubbornly to this world always, loudly insisting upon itself.

Why no one had set fire to it or the city fathers hadn't demanded that it be bulldozed to the ground was fodder for all kinds of conversations.

Virulently racist whites wanted it to remain as a reminder to black folk that what had happened here could happen again. And black people wanted it to remain for the very same reason.

Padagonia stepped down on the gas pedal and the store became a blur outside of Tass's window.

That evening, Tass baked four chicken thighs, two sweet potatoes, and made a pot of string beans. When she went to the door to call Padagonia for dinner, her friend was already climbing the porch steps. She had a beaten black pocketbook slung over her shoulder.

"Why do you have your pocketbook?"

"I plum forgot that tonight was bingo. You wanna come?"

"But I just made dinner."

"We'll eat it later."

Tass's stomach growled. "I gotta eat before I go anywhere."

Padagonia grunted, "Sorry for you then. Bingo ain't gonna wait for you to fill your belly."

"Some friend you are!" Tass cried as Padagonia turned and started back down the steps.

After dinner, Tass pulled the rocking chair out onto the porch and sat down. The street was quiet, and a placid dark sky hung overhead. She was grateful for the serenity.

A mischievous breeze wafted across her bare arms, raising goose bumps. Tass shivered. When she rose to go inside to retrieve her sweater, she saw movement in the tall grass next to Padagonia's house. Soon, a dark figure emerged.

The two stared at one another for some time, before the stranger raised a hand and waved. Tass waved back and waited for something more, but the man or woman — she couldn't tell — stepped back into the grass.

Odd, she thought. The sweater forgotten, she went into the house and prepared for bed.

CHAPTER THIRTY-SEVEN

The next day, the 28th of August, the stranger was little more than a foggy memory. Tass's focus that morning was on the backyard.

Hemmingway's once beautiful garden was now a patchwork of bald spots and weeds, and a toilet for stray cats.

As a child Tass had spent plenty of hours out there, playing house and helping her mother wash and hang the sheets. Back then, the small bit of yard was lush with vegetables and a rosebush heavy with pink blossoms.

Now, all that was left from that era were a rusted washtub, hoe, and shovel.

"I'm going to need some help with this," Tass commented aloud.

She grabbed her purse and went out to her car. Tass would take the long way to the Piggly Wiggly — she didn't want to ever lay eyes on that store again.

At the Piggly Wiggly, Tass stood behind people pushing shopping carts loaded with cases of water and canned goods. On the drive back, she passed cars with lumber and plywood tied to the roofs.

You would think it was the end of the world, Tass laughed to herself.

Later, she and Padagonia stood in the center of the yard outfitted in floppy hats, old T-shirts, and sweatpants. Scattered at their feet were vegetable seedlings, a young rosebush, a shiny new spade, and dozens of packets of flower seeds.

The sky above their heads was as clear as any I had ever seen.

"You start over there." Tass pointed to the far left of the yard. "And I'll tackle this area.

They raked, dug, pulled, and planted, and in less than an hour the two women were parched and clothes soaked with perspiration.

"Water break, boss?" Padagonia cried from her side of the yard.

Tass chuckled. "I think we both need one."

They retreated into the kitchen, where Tass filled two glasses with ice water. Padagonia drained her glass before Tass could even steal a sip from hers.

"More, please."

Outside, the crickets hummed and the horseflies buzzed in the shade.

Padagonia rubbed her belly. "You hungry?"

"I think I could eat," Tass said.

"I got tuna fish already made. How does that sound to you?"

"Just fine."

They walked across the road.

After Padagonia set the plates onto the table, she sauntered over to the television.

"Judge Judy is on."

Tass shrugged. "I guess I can watch one case."

The hours slipped by, and soon it was five o'clock. After a commercial promoting a weight-loss drink, the news came on. A pretty blue-eyed anchorwoman told the viewing audience that the top stories that evening included a hurricane which was moving rapidly into the Gulf of Mexico.

Padagonia stood up, stretched her long arms over her head, and announced that she was going to have a drink. When she opened the refrigerator door, Tass saw that it held at least eight six-packs of Pink Champale. Padagonia grabbed one six-pack from the shelf and allowed the door to swing shut. Tass turned off the television and followed her out to the porch.

The light was slowly draining from the sky. Down the street, a group of girls played hopscotch while a tight knit of boys watched. Observing the scene, Tass was suddenly flooded with a feeling of nostalgia.

Padagonia pushed a bottle at Tass. "Want one?"

Tass wasn't a drinker and at first declined, and then swiftly changed her mind. "Yes, I think I will have one." She unscrewed the top and tilted the bottle to her lips. The frothy sweetness was a pleasant surprise. "That's really good," she declared with a smack of her lips. She rolled the cold bottle across her forehead. "It sure was hot today."

"Yes, it was," Padagonia said, and then, "It's too damn quiet out here."

She disappeared into the house and came back with her transistor radio, which she set down on the windowsill.

"It's oldies night," Padagonia announced as she fiddled with the antenna.

Songs sung by Martha and the Vandellas, the Supremes, and Little Richard ushered the two women back through time.

"They don't make music like that anymore," Padagonia remarked wistfully.

"That is true."

Padagonia opened a fresh bottle of Champale, took three swigs, and then set the bottle down between her feet. Casting her eyes up and down the street, she let off a soft, satisfied sigh. "It's really very beautiful here."

"Yeah, it is."

"Good people. Christian people."

"Uh-huh."

"You would never think something so horrible happened in such a peaceful place."

Tass glanced over at her friend. "What did you say?"

Padagonia reached for the bottle. "Just thinking out loud."

They had been through it all before. Fifty years earlier, their young minds had twisted and turned with the effort of trying to understand why J.W. and Roy had done such a thing. That incident had opened up a world of horror for them. Fear and distrust surfaced where before there had been none.

J.W. and Roy didn't just snatch the childhood away from Emmett; they stole it from every single black child in Mississippi.

Why did Padagonia have to go and make that comment? Now the evening was ruined. Tass stood to leave.

"You going?"

"Yeah, I'm gonna head in."

"You want another Pink Champale?"

"No thanks."

299

"Suit yourself," Padagonia huffed.

That night, Tass dreamed she was standing on the porch in her nightgown. Once again, the dark stranger emerged from the grass and waved. Tass waved back.

The person stepped into the moonlight and Tass could see that it was a young man. Head bowed, he inched toward the curb and stopped. He seemed to be contemplating the road. He slid his foot over the edge of the sidewalk and set the toe of his shoe against the blacktop, as if testing the temperature of bathwater. Confident, he then placed his entire foot flat on the surface. The other foot followed.

He did not walk; he lumbered like an old person or a toddler taking his first steps. When he reached Tass's side of the street, he seemed winded and leaned against a nearby tree.

He must be sick, Tass thought, *or maybe drunk.*

"You all right?"

The man raised his hand and nodded.

"You sure?"

Again, the nod.

The stranger moved away from the tree and shuffled closer. He wore the night like a cape, so even in the moonlight Tass couldn't

300

make out his features.

"You need something?"

He opened his mouth, and Tass was sure she heard a swishing sound. No, not swishing, Tass thought, lapping, like water against a shore.

"Huh?" She cocked her right ear in his direction and asked if he wouldn't mind repeating himself, and this time what emanated from his mouth was a gurgle of words wrapped in fathoms of water.

Tass was growing impatient. "Speak up!" she shouted.

The boy balled his fists and Tass sensed that he was summoning strength from a deep, dark waterlogged place. Straining forward, he parted his lips and bubbled, "How you, ma'am?"

Tass leaned back in surprise. "Well," she laughed, "you don't have to scream. Can I help you with something?"

He swallowed, then pressed his hand to his throat and said, "Wanted to know if you needed any work done 'round the house."

Tass glanced at the night sky and then down the dark and quiet street. "Pretty late to be inquiring about work, don't you think?"

"Yessum."

"Your parents know you out here . . . so late?"

"Yessum."

"Step a little closer, I can't hardly see you."

The boy shuffled forward a bit.

"Closer," Tass insisted. The boy moved his feet, but he did not cover an inch of ground.

"Maybe in the yard?"

"Well, now that you mention the yard, I do need some things done." She pressed her finger against her chin. "Yeah, I think I could use some help. You wanna come back around eight or nine tomorrow morning?"

The boy shook his head no.

Tass's eyebrows cinched. "Well, what time were you thinking?"

"Tonight."

"Tonight?"

The boy nodded.

"No, no, it's gotta be nearing ten o'clock. I'm sure your parents would not appreciate you being out so late — how old are you?"

The boy thought about it and then raised his hands and splayed his fingers.

Tass thought he might be retarded. Her heart thumped for him. She straightened her spine and folded her arms across her breasts. "I got children and I sure wouldn't have allowed them to be working for no man or woman in the dead of night."

The boy's head fell forward.

"And besides, how you 'spect to see what you doing in the dark? I ain't got no light out back, you know."

The boy kept his head down.

"You go on home and come back when it's light. Whatever time suits you, I'll be here all day."

The boy didn't make a move to leave.

"Goodnight," Tass offered sternly, and turned to go inside. Her hand was on the doorknob when she realized she hadn't given her name or asked for his. When she turned back around, the boy was gone.

Chapter Thirty-Eight

When Tass woke on the morning of the 29th, the dream was still fresh in her mind. She lay in bed for a long time staring at the ceiling, wondering what, if anything, the dream meant.

Outside, the morning was steel-colored, windy, and laced with the scent of rain. When she finally decided to climb out of bed, she knew something was wrong because her feet were covered in brown dust.

Tass sat on the edge of the bed scratching her head. It didn't make sense. She had taken a bath before going to bed. Even if she had skipped that part of her daily routine, Tass rarely walked about on bare feet, and even if she did, the floors inside the house were clean enough to eat off.

It was all very bizarre.

The dream burned in her mind and Tass decided she needed to find out if she was losing her marbles.

Out the front door and down the steps, she marched right to the place where the young man had stood in her dream. The grass was flattened and when she bent over and laid her hand on the space, she found it to be wet.

Across the street Padagonia was sweeping. When she saw Tass her jaw dropped. "What the hell are you doing out here in your nightgown?"

Tass looked up and presented Padagonia with a grin she hadn't seen since they were girls.

"What you cheesing about?" Padagonia started across the street with the broom in tow. "You okay?" she asked when she and Tass were face to face.

Tass was giddy. "I dreamed that I was talking to a boy who was standing right here." She stabbed her finger at the spot. "And when I woke up this morning my feet were dirty, because the porch is dirty." Once again she pointed at the spot on the grass. "The grass is pressed in where he was standing."

Padagonia stared. "What in the world are you talking about?"

"I had this dream. Well, I thought it was a dream, but —"

Padagonia dropped the broom. "I don't

think you're feeling well, Tass." She raised a hand to her friend's forehead and checked for fever, but Tass was as cool as winter. Still, Padagonia took her back into the house and put her to bed.

Padagonia placed the kettle of water on the stove. She battled with the idea of calling Sonny. She decided that she would wait a day, just to see if Tass was suffering from grief or had truly taken leave of her senses.

When the water reached its boil, Padagonia drained it into a mug and dropped in a tea bag.

In the bedroom, Tass was sitting up, staring out of the window.

"Drink this," Padagonia said as she eased the mug into her friend's hand.

Tass held the mug up to her lips and gazed at Padagonia through the ropes of steam. "Don't look so worried," she said. "I'm fine, really, it was just a dream."

"Uh-huh," Padagonia sounded. "Drink."

Tass took a small sip.

"I'm gonna get my radio," Padagonia announced. "I'll be right back."

Outside, the street was buzzing with activity as people hurriedly loaded their cars with luggage and irreplaceable objects.

Padagonia sauntered over to one of her

neighbors and asked, "What's going on?"

The man had a stack of photo albums in his hand. His eyes rolled over her. "Ain't you heard?" he said with an air of annoyance. "Hurricane coming."

Padagonia frowned and looked up at the sky. It was gray, but the early-morning wind had died down to nothing and the birds were still chattering away in the treetops.

"Where you hear that?" she asked as she trailed the man to his car.

"The news!" The man dropped the stack of albums into the trunk of the car and slammed it shut.

"It don't look like no hurricane headed this-a-way. Maybe some hard rain, but that's all."

"I ain't taking no chances," he said, and turned his back on Padagonia's stupefied expression.

Back in Tass's house, Padagonia placed her six-pack of Pink Champale on the top shelf of the refrigerator. She plugged in the transistor radio and fiddled with the knobs and the antenna, but all she got was static, so she went in to check on Tass.

"How you doing, girl?"

Tass peeked out over the edge of the blanket. "A little sleepy," she yawned.

"Uh-huh. I'm gonna make us something to eat, okay?"

"Okay."

In the kitchen, Padagonia opened the refrigerator and removed a bottle of Champale, unscrewed the top, and took a swig. It was nowhere near noon, but under the circumstances Padagonia felt that God would forgive her this one little indiscretion.

After her drink, she returned to the refrigerator and surveyed its contents. She decided on eggs, bacon, and grits. After laying the strips of bacon in the pan, Padagonia went to the window and peered out and found that the clouds had turned dark in the little time it took the bacon to crisp.

While Padagonia was in the kitchen removing the bacon from the frying pan, Tass was curled under the blankets, wrapped in slumber, searching for the night boy with the water voice.

This time, when he appeared, the sun was up and she could see him quite clearly. Young, dark, full-bellied, and smiling. From the porch, she raised her hand in greeting and did not suppress the urge to run to him. It took forever — the space between them seemed to stretch for miles — and when she finally reached him, she was fifteen-and-a-quarter years old and the gown she wore was too long and too big for her.

"Hi," she said.

"Hi," he responded, and extended his hand.

Tass took it and they started down the street.

"Where are we going?"

"You'll see," he said.

Tass gathered the skirt of her gown and began to skip. The boy laughed and joined in. They skipped all the way to Bryant's grocery store. Tass stopped and the hem of her gown slipped from her hands.

The boy turned to her. "What's wrong?"

"I can't go in there."

"Why?"

Tass couldn't remember why and so she said, "I don't know, I just know I can't."

The boy said, "Okay. Wait here." And strolled up to the door, pulled it open, and stepped in. He returned carrying two grape ice pops and handed her one.

"For me?" Tass gushed.

"There's a gobstopper in it."

"I bet you I can beat you to the middle," Tass said as she peeled the paper away from the pop.

"No bites, just licks," the boy declared.

"What's the prize?"

He glanced down the road and then bashfully back to Tass. "A kiss?"

Tass blushed. "Do I know you?"

"Yes, you do," he said, and took her hand again.

"What's your name?"

"My friends call me Bobo."

"Bobo?" Tass rolled the name around her mouth. "I think I do remember you," she said, and took a lick of her ice pop.

Padagonia walked to the front door and pulled it open. She spied a calico streaking down the middle of the street ahead of her litter. The trees were silent — which meant the birds had fled. Other than the cats, there didn't seem to be a speck of life around.

She began to feel unsettled and unsure. Her eyes rolled up to the sky and then over to her Pacer. *Perhaps,* she thought as she gently shut the door, *we should leave. Just to be safe.*

"Tass," Padagonia called as she made her way to the bedroom. "I'm thinking it might be a good idea to head someplace other than here."

In the bedroom the curtains were flapping and billowing like sails against the open window.

"What in the world?" Padagonia cried as she reached to close the window. The sky cracked open and rain fell in hard, clear drops.

Tass's cell phone began to chime. Padagonia looked and saw that it was Sonny calling.

"Tass, wake up, your phone is ringing."

She was about to walk over to the bed to shake her friend awake when she spotted two young people coming up the road. The girl was dressed in what looked to be a nightgown; the boy wore a pair of cutoff shorts and a T-shirt. They were holding hands, licking ice pops, and strolling as if the day was dry, clear, and bright.

When they reached the lot, Padagonia pushed her head out into the downpour and yelled, "Hey, you two, watch out now, there are snakes in that grass!"

The couple turned around and Padagonia strained to make out their faces. They beckoned with their hands, "Come on, come with us!"

"Go home and get out of this rain!" Padagonia closed the window and went to Tass. "Get up, I think we need to leave."

Tass did not move. Padagonia pulled back the blanket and gave her shoulder a good, firm shake.

"Tass?"

Before Tass and Emmett skipped off into forever, *she* had started to form over the Bahamas, a tropical depression — an annoyance at best. Cunning and slick, careful to appear unthreatening, *she* slipped into Florida without raising an eyebrow. The meteorologist didn't think enough of her to even give her a pretty name.

In the Gulf of Mexico, *she* suddenly turned furious. Draped in black clouds, blowing wind, and driving rain, *she* charged into Louisiana like a bull and fanned her billowing dark skirts over Mississippi.

They named her Katrina, but I looked into the eye of that storm and recognized her for who she really was: Esther the whore, cackling and clapping her hands with glee.

Whether you have embraced this tale as truth or fantasy, I hope you will take something away from having read it. I pray that you will become more sensitive to the world around you, the seen and unseen. As you go about your lives, keep in mind that an evil act can ruin generations, and gestures of love and kindness will survive and thrive forever.

Choose wisely, dearest . . .

Light,
Money Mississippi

GRATITUDE . . .

I am grateful to God, my guides, ancestors, family, and friends.

A special thanks to: Carlo and Quovardis Lawrence and family, who opened their home and hearts for me to climb the steepest part of the mountain which ultimately became this book; Mrs. Anita Abbott, who is mother and friend to me; my sister, Misty McFadden, who encouraged me forward and continued to believe in me when I found it difficult to believe in myself; Terry McMillan — for too many reasons to list; new friends Amy Moore, Alicia McMillan, and Joyce McMillan, who keep me thinking and laughing.

Special thanks to my spiritual siblings: Andrea Knight, Darlene Harden, and Eric Payne, who have loved and supported me over the years; and to my publisher Johnny Temple and the fabulous staff at Akashic

Books, who allow me to publish with dignity.

And you readers — I am especially grateful to have you in my life.

Emmett Till — you did not die in vain!

Love there,
Bernice L. McFadden